Crunch

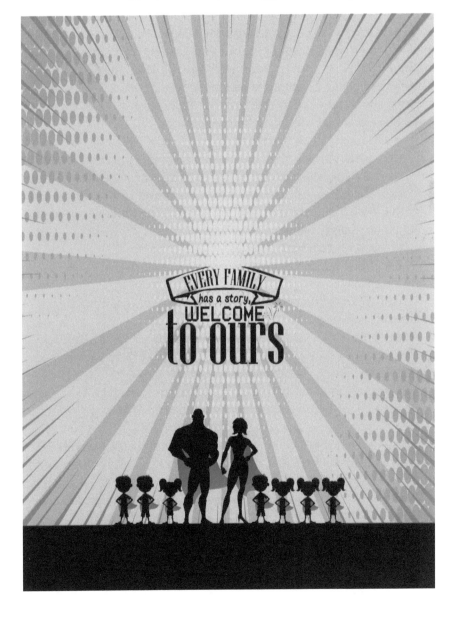

Introduction

For many years I've wanted to write a Super-Hero book, but for the life of me I could never figure out how I should do it. I was initially inspired by the first round of Marvel movies, but then they just kept making them, and I abandoned the idea for years because there was just so many Super-Hero movies around that I couldn't see how you could make one that was totally unique and original.

Finally, I came up with an idea.

There were a few movies that helped spurn the idea that follows. The first was a single line from *The Incredibles 2*. Mr. incredible is working with another Super-Hero, and in the movie Mr. Incredible asks this other hero if he can undo what he just did. The other Super-Hero looks at him and says with a confuzzled look:

"Can you un-punch somebody?"

I heard the line and thought to myself . . . hmm. I think there might be an idea.

Then the other movie that contributed to this book was a Disney Movie called *Sky High*.

It's a unique movie about a Super-Hero high-school, and in the movie (to make a long story short) all the people at this party get turned into babies for a short while.

Ever since I've seen that movie, I've thought to myself, *'Man, they could have an interesting movie if they did it just a little bit different.'*

You'll understand what I mean later.

Then as I got thinking more seriously about the idea, I wondered what would normal everyday life would look like for a Super-Hero. And if you were to have a Super-Hero tell you his life story, what would he tell you? The result is a satirical comedy, and I certainly hope you enjoy it!

Crunch

A Super-Hero Story

Tyler Svec

Crunch

This novel is a work of fiction. Names, descriptions, entities, and incidents
included in the story are products of the author's imagination. Any
resemblance to actual persons, events and entities is entirely coincidental.

Cover Art courtesy of shutterstock.com
Cover Design by Tyler Svec
Interior Design by Tyler Svec

Softcover ISBN: # 987-1-387-45937-7

Furthermore, I've always wanted to write a book from the perspective of a first person narrative. It was a bit of work but a lot of fun to write.

Also I would like to thank my wife and kids who were always able to help me come up with funny things to put in the story.

So without further ado, I present to you Walter Braymend, or as you'll soon know him a Super-Hero named, 'Crunch'.

Chapter 1

Life for me has been different. Really different. Imagine the strangest life you've ever heard of, and then multiply that by ten and you might come close to the life that I've lived. It's not a bad life, don't get me wrong, just unusual.

You know what, let's back up and start again, because I got this totally wrong.

Okay, here we go . . .

Hi, my name is Walter Braymend. I'm now 40 years old. I have a wife and seven kids.

That was better, right? Probably doesn't sound too freaky, which is good. I know some people reading are like, holy crap! Seven kids. Just wait. It gets better.

(Side-note: seven kids has been really fun.)

Okay, sorry. Won't get distracted again, at least I'll try not to.

I'm Walter Braymend, and I am a Super-Hero.

Now before you go and start thinking—*Oh, that's so cool! A Super-Hero! A real life Super-Hero!*—it's not all it's cracked up to be,

Crunch

and it is nothing like the movies or comic books. Those shouldn't even be allowed to be published.

Ah! They're just embarrassing.

I figure (for starters) it's only fitting if I explain a little bit about what *actual* Super-Heroes are like, compared to what you've probably seen in movies and comic books. We'll start with some things that are true.

Firstly, the code-names are real. It only makes sense right? Protects our identity. However, we don't get to choose our names. When we graduate from Super-Hero school, we are brought before a large council called *Super-Hero Association of Naming Council Tactical Innovation Offensive Nuances.* It's quite a mouthful, but it's an acronym. (Our government loves acronyms, too.)

It's lovingly referred to as S.A.N.C.T.I.O.N. That's partially due to the fact that not to many people even know what the acronym stands for, or even care. The council is made of up 937 Super-Heroes. And there is always a select member of the Super-Hero community that is kept in reserve in case they should come to a tie.

I'm not sure under what circumstances 937 people would 'tie' a vote on anything . . . mathematically it's impossible.

But rules are rules!

The point is that this council (made up of 937 Super-Heroes) looks at your file and your abilities, and then they choose your name. They do take suggestions from friends and family, but those are rarely accepted. S.A.N.C.T.I.O.N. usually insists on unique names.

So, sometimes you get a cool name like Ice Man or Rocky; then there's other times you get named after the dumbest things you've done.

For example . . .

I knew a guy whose name was Mac. His code-name was 'Cheese'.

Tyler Svec

His power didn't even have anything to do with cheese. But still he was called Cheese for the rest of his Super-Hero days. I don't know how he put up with it. I would find that rather embarrassing, and no pun intended, it would be very 'cheesy'.

Okay, the pun was totally intended. How could it not be? 'Hey! Can we get some *Cheese* on that pizza?' 'Hey *Cheese,* are you from Wisconsin?' The possibilities are endless.

Sorry, staying focused.

Other notable names that are funny: Skid-Mark. Gopher. Soxs. My personal favorite in the funny category was Mr. Bubble Butt. Named so because, during his sophomore year at his Super-Hero school, he attempted to jump off a building, with a large roll of bubble wrap taped to his butt.

His Super-Power was reversing physics, so he could stop himself before he actually hit the ground if he wanted to. He was never actually in *that* much danger. Or in any danger, if you think about it. However, that being said the bubble wrap reacted differently to his Super-Power than he intended, and he sent himself soaring nearly three hundred feet into the air . . . and into a power line.

Therefore, on his name day he became Mr. Bubble Butt, and the rest of us never get tired of those jokes.

Never.

I actually have a pretty descent name, all things considered. My name is Crunch, because I can crunch stuff. That's my Super-Power. Crunching things. If it won't fit, ask me.

I'll make it fit.

Oops, did you measure your door wrong? The dishwasher won't fit?

Let me at it. Two seconds later it'll be the size of a monopoly dice. Problem solved.

Crunch

At least partially.

I've never quite mastered how to crunch things, and have them be lighter. When I was fifteen I was out on the town with some friends, and they dared me to crunch a semi-truck . . .

So I did.

It looked like a Hot Wheels car. It was pretty awesome. But I couldn't pick it up for the life of me. At the time it was the most frustrating thing because you know someone's going to notice that a semi-truck just went missing, and all you're trying to do is put in your pocket, so you can put it on your shelf as a trophy.

That day I learned there are some limits to 'crunching' things. For one, they retain the weight of the un-crunched item. So back to the whole dishwasher scenario, (which may or may not have happened.) It might be the size of a dice, but it still has the weight of a full sized dishwasher.

Okay, it was our neighbors dishwasher and I 'accidentally' crunched it.

It was a couple of weeks until they talked to us again.

I bought them a new one.

They like us now. Mostly.

I know most of you are thinking, just 'un-crunch the item!'

Sorry, I don't un-crunch things. That's not my specialty. I . . . I just don't do that.

Not that I won't do it, because that just makes me sound lazy, but . . .

Okay, so here's the things with Super-Powers; they have their limits. I can crunch stuff, but I *can't* un-crunch stuff. No matter how hard I try I will never be able to un-crunch something. You might be saying to yourself 'well that's lame.'

It totally is, but that's how God made me.

Tyler Svec

You see, unlike what you see in movies, there are two sides to every 'save the day moment.' There are Crunchers like me, and there are un-Crunchers. When you graduate you are paired with a person whose Super-Power is the opposite of yours. It's mostly done this way to hide the fact that we were there at all.

Let's face it, people get pretty upset at you if you come in and destroy all their things. Sure you may catch the bad guys, but you just leveled thirty-nine buildings in the process.

Good for you.

See you in court.

The insurance companies also would be pretty upset at us.

If Superman was actually real he would have gotten his butt sued so much in court that even his spandex would refuse to show itself in public ever again. For which, this half of the world would say 'Thank you!'

I've never been a fan of 'Superman' but that's probably okay because he's not . . . real. He's a movie. Seriously he has, like, every Super-Power you could ever think of, and still he destroys everything and . . .

I'm getting off track.

Back to my point, that's why there's always two. A Cruncher and a un-Cruncher. However, in my case I was never actually paired with an un-Cruncher, but that's getting ahead of the story.

Where was I?

Myths about Super-Heroes. Right.

Along with Code-names, we do have Super Suits. They are really uncomfortable!

You're basically wearing industrial strength spandex. It feels like you're walking around in a suit of armor that's skin tight.

We don't get to choose the color of those, either. Regrettably.

Crunch

That's left up to S.A.N.C.T.I.O.N. So 'Cheese' naturally had a suit that looked like it was covered in slices of cheddar cheese. Bubble Butt, had a super suit-

You know, you don't need to know what his suit looked like . . .

It might have had bright red dots on the butt . . . might have.

Whoever designed my super suit, must have been color blind because it's bright yellow. I look like a flippin' school bus, and then if that wasn't enough to make you cringe, I have a dark purple "C" written on the front and back of the suit. It's really hard to sneak into anyplace with a suit like that, but hey, when I have it on, people know it's me who's there to save the day . . . so I guess it's okay.

But still, yellow?

Why couldn't it have been black or deep blue. I'd even settle with a maroon red? But, no, yellow.

Next thing that is true, based on what you've seen of Super-Heroes, is that the stupid, pointless disguises actually *do* work.

Somehow in the movies, the very fact that Clark Kent can wear glasses and nobody recognizes him is true. I, for example, have a mustache that I wear. I'm usually a clean shaven guy, because my wife can't stand facial hair. But when I'm in my super suit, I have a big bushy mustache that goes on as well.

For one of my Super-Hero friends, whose name is Plug, the only thing he does is put on a different T-Shirt. I've never figured out how that works because it's the same color T-shirt! He always (and I do mean always!) wears a black T-Shirt.

Never a different color.

He claims he has two, one for work and one for causal. He will carry the other shirt around on a hanger with him, literally everywhere (so it doesn't get wrinkled). When he gets the call, he slips on the *other* shirt, and before he's even in his super suit, (which conveniently was designed so his t-shirt is visible) everyone recognizes him.

Oh, and just so you know there are three classes of Super-Heroes. They are officially called A, B, and C class, but those are boring names and nobody really uses those.

At least most don't.

Okay, I don't.

First and foremost, there is the 'Class A' Super-Heroes, which I affectionately call 'Freaks.'

Some of them have, like, twenty-seven Super-Powers. Who needs that many Super-Powers?

Now naturally, the people who have that many Super-Powers are sent to another school and don't need to have someone else with them on assignments, so they get first dibs on all the really cool missions . . .

I'm a little bitter about that.

I've only met one Class A Super-Hero that didn't have an ego the size of a building, and that was a guy whose name was 'Snake King'. He was a huge guy, plenty scary to look at. He had tattoos up and down his arms, muscles coming out of everywhere! Freaky-looking hair, and he wore a tank-top and bandanna.

Oh, and he had an eye-patch!

I've wanted to get an eye-patch for a while, but my wife says I don't need one.

That might be true, but don't you think that just gives your persona a bit of an edge? Makes you look tougher?

Anyway, the Snake King was a cool guy, because although he looked tough, you know what he did for a day job?

Worked in a greenhouse.

His parents had been big on gardening, and it rubbed off on him.

His wife thinks it's great, too, because they get discounted prices on all the plants she could ever want. They have like the biggest garden you've ever seen.

So, yeah, he's cool, because he works a normal job, and is actually a very soft spoken guy, but when he needs to be he can turn himself into a fire shooting, mind piercing, acid trailing snake that will strike terror into bad guys everywhere.

Next, there is 'Class B' Super-Hero's. This is the class I'm in, so naturally I think it's the best.

People like me have only one Super-Power. Hence, my crunching. So we go to a special school to better learn how to use our one Super-Power and are trained to be completely efficient in that one Super-Power.

Also, I should explain that there is a difference between Super-Strength and Crunching. Super-Strength you can pick up items of immense size, rip cars in half, things of that nature.

I can't do that.

I crunch them, so I literally fold them in on themselves using mostly my mind. So I suppose when I use my power, I look like I'm Luke Skywalker using the force.

After that there is the 'Class C' Super-Hero's, and they are usually referred to as 'Tinkers'. They also have only one Super-Power, but it's usually deemed a pretty useless Super-Power. They're still trained to be efficient in it, but they're unlikely to see any serious 'action'.

An example of a 'Class C' Super-Power would be a guy named "Lever."

He's very, very good at making one thing . . . levers!

He can make them out of anything, and he has even been on a few high profile jobs, but mostly he sits at home and practices making levers.

Now it is important to note that just because you are a Class C

Tyler Svec

Super-Hero does not mean you will always be Class C. Sometimes your ability is in high demand or the situation calls for it. Sometimes, you become so good in your ability that you get upgraded.

For example there was a guy named "Buttons." He was very good at making buttons. Not like the buttons on your shirt, but like buttons on a control board. It took him about ten years for him to learn how to attach them to an existing circuit board, but he eventually did.

As a result he got upgraded to a Class B.

How better to turn off a nuclear reactor then being able to make a button that's connected in such a way that you can actually turn it off.

Pretty handy, if you ask me.

Another misconception of Super-Heroes is that we somehow have gained our power, by divine intervention or something of the sort.

Couldn't be further from the truth. We're not aliens, we're not gods, we're not super freaks or lab experiments. We are just like you . . . except cooler.

I'm just kidding.

But seriously, it does all come down to inheriting the 'super' genes. If there's a Super-Hero in your family tree anywhere, then you are carrying the super gene, and any one of your descendants could become a Super-Hero.

I let you know that because it's a common myth that if you don't have direct Super-Hero parents than you're never going to be a Super-Hero.

So, I know you're going to have heard various movie characters having a super serum like *Captain America.* But it's all not true.

Now, just to dispel the murmurs I hear going through your mind right now . . . there is one case that may fit with what you see in movies.

My wife was the daughter of missionaries in the Philippines. They

Crunch

have no known family history of being in the line of Super-Heroes, yet she gained Super-Powers.

How?

That's the real question isn't it.

In the official intake report it is written (and she will swear by the truth of the statement) that she was bitten by a Cordellian Spider Snake . . .

Have you ever heard of a Cordellian Spider Snake?

I haven't.

For years, I've looked up everything I can find on weird animals, but I've never found anything on the existence of a Cordellian Spider Snake!

What is Cordellian? Let alone a Spider Snake?! Is it a snake with legs?

Is Cordellian some long lost Latin word for . . . I'm not even sure what it would stand for.

Correction?

Cordially?

Lian?

Between you and me, I think she made it up.

But whether she did or she didn't get bit by a Cordellian Spider Snake, or she has some ancestor way, way back who had the super gene, who really knows? It doesn't prove your theory and it doesn't quite prove mine, but it could be either . . .

Although my theory is a little more likely.

There! You have the basics, now let's move on.

Chapter 2

So, let me tell you. Being a child is hard enough. But when you put the whole notion of Super-Powers in the mix, that is something else altogether.

Now for the kid it's great fun, and we hardly realize the embarrassing, awkward situations we create.

Because we're kids, and we don't think about stuff like that.

However, having been on the other side of that equation, as I've been a parent now for a number of years, I can honestly say it is . . .

Annoying.

Yeah, annoying is definitely the best word.

Imagine if you will, you're sitting down to eat supper at a nice Burger King restaurant . . .

Okay, hang on, back it up.

Before we continue on, it should be noted that 'Super-Kids' eat a TON of food! Easily three times the normal amount, at lunch and supper.

At breakfast they eat hardly anything.

Crunch

I haven't figured that out yet.

Maybe we should have taken our kids out to eat at breakfast time. It would've been a whole lot more economical.

So, the Burger King restaurant.

You're there with your wife and seven very young kids and you've just ordered fifty-two orders of fries, three burgers for each kid, and a salad.

Put in that order next time you're at any restaurant and see what kind of reactions you get. I don't even think it qualifies as shock, I think it goes beyond shock, to 'stunned silence.' Usually they stand there looking like they've been watching golf for four hours, and then they look at you funny and ask—

'Sorry, sir, what was your order?'

HELLO! I just told you. I want everything I just told you, *and* throw in a vanilla shake, please!

Again, you'll be met by stunned silence.

About then you're getting impatient (and slightly embarrassed) and you think you're going to have to wave your hand in front of their face and say in your best Obi-Wan Kenobi voice, *'You want to take our order!'*

Finally, the shock wears off and they take your order, smiling awkwardly and reply with *'I'm sorry sir, I thought I had heard you wrong. Are you expecting more people?'*

Yes.

Yes, I am.

And then you sit down and eat your food as quickly, (but politely) as you can, and then leave before anyone notices.

We really tried not to go out to eat that often . . . and if we did, we tried not to go to the same restaurant more than once.

We actually got banned from one place when our kids were

teenagers.

It wasn't even a real restaurant.

It was our oldest daughters birthday (she was turning 15 at the time) and so we ask, *Where would you like to go out for dinner?* She was big on salads at the time. So she chose this place called the 'Salad Bar'. It only served salad.

And Dr. Pepper.

Of course, they had water too.

But literally, the only kind of other drink they had was Dr. Pepper! Does anybody even drink Dr. Pepper?

Not I, says Walter Braymend!

Anyway, this *lovely* restaurant had to close early because they ran out of . . . pretty much everything. They accused us of wasting good food as they seemed to think we were throwing it away.

No. I just have seven EXTREMELY hungry teenage Super-Kids thank you!

I didn't actually say that.

I wanted to though.

Instead, I just smiled dumbly and told the truth . . . 'We ate it all.'

They didn't believe us and threatened to get a restraining order or sue us if we came back . . .

It's really okay, I'm not that big on salad.

Actually, fun fact, meat is the best thing for a Super-Hero diet.

My wife and I talked about going Amish and raising our own cows, because of how much meat we consumed as a family. We never did, but life would've been so much easier if we had.

Imagine that. Amish Super-Kids! Wouldn't that mess with some people?

Yep, we have a horse and buggy, and Super-Powers!

Once I met a girl, and she had some Super-Power where she could

Crunch

make things go faster. That would be amazing.

So we have a horse a buggy, but it can still outrun your Ferrari! And then after that, one of the kids could become a jockey and we can place winning bets on all the races and we'd be . . .

Never-mind, that's getting a little sidetracked.

It's hard because sometimes the rabbit trails are just so much fun to go down.

Speaking of rabbits. My wife and I raise these rabbits, and they're like twenty pounds a piece!

Never-mind.

As a kid I'm sure I made my parents just as embarrassed or awkward as mine did to me. But once again, as a kid you don't think about it.

The first time I remember using my Super-Power, I made my best friend cry. Accidentally of course. I was five, and I was at his birthday party (his name was Jasper). He had just gotten this nice new toy truck. It was red, and had lights and made sounds.

Super cool.

It was his idea to line up at the end of his hallway and send the truck cruising down the hallway, while trying to hit it with one of the other cars that he had.

Seems like a harmless idea, until a young Mr. Crunch got a hold of the other car.

When I launched it down the hallway I was thinking to myself 'what if it got damaged like a real car?'

Wish granted.

They collided and both of them were quickly reduced to crumpled heaps of plastic.

My friend was not happy.

I, on the other hand, was jumping up and down like I had won the

Tyler Svec

lottery. I didn't really think about the situation at the time; I was just thrilled that something 'super' had happened.

The truly amazing thing was, they were actually smoking as though they had been real cars! I remember wishing they would catch fire or explode like you would see in the movies.

Okay, so I hadn't seen movies with that kind of stuff in them at that point in time . . . because I was five. But I still wished they could catch fire. Sadly though, they didn't.

Just to prove how much I didn't realize I had screwed up, I asked my friend if I could have the cars.

He cried harder.

So I stuffed them in my backpack and still have them in a box somewhere in our attic.

Okay! So, technically I stole them, but it was pretty clear that Jasper wasn't going to be playing with them ever again. His parents were openly talking about buying him a new toy car. So they weren't going to miss them.

Looking back, I'm not exactly sure how my dad smoothed things over with his parents. I was too excited to care. That was how my Super-Hero journey started.

There are various kinds of crunching I've learned to do since then. I can make it look really bad. Or as I can crunch it, it'll keep the shape and not be damaged, but it'll be miniature and keep the weight of the original object.

Looking back now, I feel like the destructive crunching caused more stress and strife for my parents.

I can take any sports car or armored vehicle and make it look like its been through a demolition derby.

I got us in trouble once when I was six. We were going car shopping and for whatever reason, every car I walked by was reduced

Crunch

into a junk heap.

The awesome thing about that was I wasn't even trying to destroy it. I just did.

Once again, I felt awesome, and I have no idea how Dad got us out of that.

The next day though, Dad arranged for us to go over to his friends junkyard after hours. He was a Super-Hero too, so he understood the situation. There I could practice and it didn't matter what I crunched because it was all going to be recycled anyway.

Other interesting memories . . . ah, yes . . .

There was one time, I sent one of my babysitters to the hospital.

It was an accident, albeit a funny one. She had stepped out of the room for two seconds, to talk to her boyfriend on the phone and I wanted some ketchup.

I grabbed the bottle and that was that.

Really little bottle, but the ketchup didn't shrink with it.

Cue the big explosion! There was ketchup everywhere.

It looked like a war zone, plus I had it all over my face and arms. Long story short, she comes in, goes into a panicked frenzy, dials 911, goes unconscious...

Next thing I know there are police, firefighters, and an ambulance all in our front yard!

The babysitter went to the hospital for mild concussion symptoms.

She never babysat for us again, which is too bad, I actually liked her.

A whole lot nicer than Julia. I wish I could've crunched fifty bottles of ketchup on her.

Ugh!

In my young age, it seemed to be only when I got really excited about something that it would get crunched. I could walk up and down the food aisle in Wal-Mart for twenty years and nothing would happen. Put me in a toy store, watch out. For a while we didn't go to toy stores, because of the incidents I created.

For example: walking by Legos.

Box and Legos would shrink down to the size of a dice. With as small as some pieces are these days I can't imagine trying to put one of those together.

I'm not sure if it would be worth it or not.

'Hey, friends! Look at my cool three thousand piece fighter jet Lego set that can fit in the palm of your hand!'

Crunchers like myself usually get employed in the packing and shipping business, as a day job, because that's a very natural thing for us. We can shrink the object, just a little, to fit in that box . . .

I've never worked in shipping, or packing.

I worked at a book printing facility, just a few miles outside of town.

Ever wonder where the pocket sized version of books came from? You can thank me for that.

The higher-ups were lamenting about costs and how they wish they could do it cheaper . . . one quick crunch later and everyone was happy.

The only problem was, I had crunched the machine to make smaller books, which made getting parts and ink much harder. Actually impossible.

It took a few years for the technology to catch up with what I had done. But it's all better now.

I got a raise as a result of my creation.

Pinatas were another thing that were outlawed for a while.

I was at another friend's birthday party and they had a pinata. The girl took one swing at it and the pinata was reduced to the size of a

Crunch

tack, meanwhile all the candy stayed the same and flew everywhere. Some of it went up to a half mile away.

She was standing there in shock while everyone else was yelling excitedly trying to get the candy. It's really amazing that I had any friends growing up.

Family vacations were always an adventure, too.

We went to San-Francisco when I was eight. You should have seen my face when I saw the Golden Gate Bridge.

Ah! It was a wonderful sight, all that steel and concrete, just begging to be crunched! My father saw the look in my eye and very swiftly put that to an end.

Thanks, Dad.

As I got older I was steadily growing in my ability to control my crunching. That being said, sometimes I did things just for fun . . . because why not?

Ever been to a sports store? Somewhere in the store, they have a huge bin of basketballs—you know the kind. They were in this large wire cage and would only come out the bottom . . .

And then I came walking through the store.

Watch this everyone!

Moment's later all the basketballs were shrunk to the size of bouncy balls.

They bounced really good, but remember what I said about them keeping the weight of the object no matter the size? That should have popped into my head at the time, but it didn't.

The whole experience turned out to be one of the more dangerous stunts I've pulled. By the time the last of the shrunken basketballs had stopped bouncing, there were holes in walls, the front door on the store was shattered, a couple of cars were damaged. Shelves were knocked over . . .

Tyler Svec

I never did it again.

My parents were saints. For years I never knew how they put up with all the things I did. Now that I'm a parent it really comes down to the fact that you just love your kids so much that you're able to eventually overlook those kinds of moments.

Upside—you have lots of memories to laugh at when you're old.

Chapter 3

Fast-forward now to when I entered seventh grade.

Just so you know, seventh grade is the grade every Super-Kid dreams about because this is the year you finally get to go to Super-Hero school.

You might be asking, 'Well, why do you not go to Super-School right away?'

The simple answer is the teachers already have a hard enough job, trying to teach junior high/high school to Super-Kids. If you were to have a Super-Kid's elementary school the building would probably be destroyed by the end of the first day, because we don't know how to control anything. The idea is by this stage in life, you've figured out how to control your Super-Power, at least a little.

And just so you know, it's about five percent of the population that are Super-Heroes. So although it is still a lot of people, it's not like everyone and their dog is a Super-Hero.

There have been people who have tried to bring their dogs to Super-School though; they aren't allowed.

Tyler Svec

There's a few higher ups that are allergic to pet hair, so if you by chance have one of those therapy dogs, you're out of luck.

Someone once brought a therapy goldfish with them. That was strange, but no pet hair, so it was allowed.

Just imagine this future Super-Hero carrying around a bag with a goldfish in it.

It was only fitting that when the kid graduated, he was given the code-name, 'Jumbo Shrimp'.

Now, I know there have been lots of TV shows or movies about Super-Hero schools. Some are more right than others. But know this: our school doesn't fly (which is kind of disappointing). It's not some secret portal that we step into and we're there. There are several communities around the world that are basically covers for Super-Schools.

The year before, you have to go visit the Super-Hero headquarters to get evaluated.

Now I know you probably want to know where that is, but I can't tell you.

That is strictly confidential.

I could tell you, but then I'd have to kill you . . .

Which is why I'm not going to do it, because I *would* have to kill you, and I can't possibly do that through a book.

Bam! You're dead!

See, didn't work. You're still reading.

Moving on.

The summer before, you are brought in and are placed in front of S.A.N.C.T.I.O.N. As well as the Super-Hero Intake Coordination Koalition. (S.I.C.K.)

It's a horrible acronym, but it's government. I think they spelled Coalition wrong on purpose just so it would make a word, otherwise it

Crunch

would be the SICC (Phonetically, I think that would be SA-IS-SSS.)

Just doesn't have the same ring to it.

Long story short, there are close to nine different agencies that are involved in determining where you get to go to school. Like I told you previously, there are three different classes A, B, and C. All three train at different areas.

So you come, you do enough interviews to make you want to hurl, and then you have to perform your Super-Power in front of all the assembly at the end of the week.

Thirty-three days later, you get a notice in the mail informing you of your class and where you'll be attending school.

You do have to report three weeks before school starts and re-perform your Super-Power.

It's almost like a re-evalutaion to see if you need to be assigned a different class. It's kind of rare that things change, but it does happen.

There was a guy, same age as me. He could create and control particles! (We all named him Particle Man)

I heard he even managed to control 2.3596 million protons in their raw, ultra-radiated bio-secular phase at the same time!

Never been done before.

One year later, he couldn't even reheat his coffee. He had clearly been playing to many video games and eating to much junk food, because he was the size of a house.

That might be a stretch, but he was certainly the size of a bear.

A big bear, without fur.

Almost like a bear who had been electrocuted, because obviously he didn't have the appearance of the bear, just the size.

Point of the story . . . you can get demoted.

And it might sound like the Super-Hero world is discriminating, but you have to be physically fit if you're going to be a Super-Hero.

Tyler Svec

We're going to be saving the world. We can't be slow.

We have to move like lightning!

It is actually impossible to move that fast, but you know what I'm saying.

Myself, being a Class B Super-Hero, meant that I qualified for the Super-Hero school in section 7. (Super-Hero maps have the worlds divided into 37 sections.) Only the Super-Heroes from *that* section can respond to calls in that section. You can be called on to join any mission, but 'home' section Super-Heroes get first dibs.

Super-Schools are set up like boarding schools, because it's unrealistic to expect every family to be able to move everything there, when you take into consideration secret sanctums, underground labs, other-worldy energy sources, things like that.

Plus, like I said with the sections . . . your parents have a responsibility to that section.

If they all moved it would be like 'So long section 17! Nice knowing you.'

Oh yeah, fun fact: we don't have a section 13.

There are some really superstitious people on the Board of Directors. (B.O.D. as we call them.)

We also don't have a section 10.

So, the maps for the sections were drawn up back in the medieval ages, and I guess they *did* have a section 10 on the map.

But then the cartographer spilled his coffee, which smeared the ink in that spot on the map.

For whatever reason, he never fixed it and it got submitted that way.

300 years later, someone finally realized the mistake and you know what? No one cared.

So section 9 is twice the size of every other section in the world

Crunch

because of it. Section 9 is coincidentally over the Pacific Ocean, which sounds like the best place to have a section that's twice as big, because there's nothing there, right?

Wrong!

Section 9 is notorious for Super-Villains who specialize in sea monsters, bio-hydrothermal detonators, and Integrated Volcanic Shipping Mechanisms.

Don't feel bad if you have no idea what any of those are, because I don't know . . . and frankly I don't care.

I'm in section 22. We don't have to deal with crap like that.

Just a side note—the world section map is not arranged in numerical order, which is why no one noticed and no one really cares that there is no section 10. Instead, all the sections were arranged by alphabetical order of the original leader of the sections in relation to where they lived at the time when the maps were drawn . . .

This is when I point out that governments never make sense. Alphabetical order, but there's only 26 letters and there are 37 sections.

I stand corrected. 35 sections. Because 2 of them are not on the map.

My bad.

Super-Heroes might save the day, but I admit, some of us really have a few screws loose.

Now that we've thoroughly discussed maps and sections, let's talk about actual school. We all arrive about a week early for orientation and go through more interviews, and then you're shown to your room. Nothing is going to be taught for a week, so the first week that you're there is to really get comfortable with the people and facilities, and dream about being a Super-Hero.

There are very specific rules about what you can't do during that first week. You're not allowed to use your Super-Power in any way. This is due to the fact that there are lots of people coming and going and not everyone is a Super-Hero and we can't risk giving the secret away to Uncle Jimmy who's unsuspectingly bringing a Super-Kid to a new school.

I'll pause to say something that's probably obvious, but I need to say it anyway. You don't just tell people you're a Super-Hero. That would be very dangerous. So the government helps hide us, and we do our best to hide ourselves without help. This is where the stupid, but useful, disguises come in handy.

But if you're a first year, no one has a flippin' clue who you are, so what does it matter?

There I said it. Let's move on.

In order to fully keep the guise that you are a normal school and not a Super-School, most of the buildings that you see are filled with normal things. We have to take both normal classes and super classes to keep up with this charade.

Beneath every building is a secret building, and subsequent tunnels connect everything.

And that's where the fun stuff is.

Take whatever you thought about Super-Hero caves and multiply it by five thousand and one. To even access the Super-School, you have to have a special ID and perform a retinal scan . . .

It's awesome! You feel so legit the first time the guard asks you for your ID, looks at it carefully and then says 'You must be new here!'

His name is Bart, and he's awesome.

His disguise is a janitor.

But he actually *is* a janitor! He has some awesome things hidden away in that mop bucket.

If he needs to, he can totally wipe the floor with you . . . every pun intended. He has one mop that can turn into a mace, one that can turn into nun-chucks, and my favorite is a mop who's handle is capable of sending twenty thousand volts of electricity into a person . . .

I saw him do that on one guy; turned out he was a Super-Villain named Little Hammer, but the best part was his power was spraying water from his finger tips. (He later confessed that he was supposed to fry all of our electrical circuits.)

Joke was on him.

The only one who got his circuits blown was Little Hammer, who was stopped with twenty thousand volts of electricity . . .

Think about it for a moment. Spraying water? Inhuman amounts of electricity? That had to hurt.

But he lived to tell the tale, and now no student or staff dare mess with or even tease Bart.

Super Classes happen at different times for different grades, just like any school would, with the rotation and all of that. These buildings are built special for the kind of things that go on beneath the surface.

Beneath the surface, life is pretty much as would be expected for being in a Super-school. The biggest difference is unlike most cafeteria food, the food at Super-School is surprisingly tasty. Again, they don't even serve breakfast because no one eats it.

It runs on a rotation and the schedule is meant to serve the needs of every student.

There's not enough meat in the diet for my liking.

The worst day is salad day. Now if you're Super-Power has anything to do with plants or agriculture than you would be very glad for this day, because it's common knowledge that it helps conduct your plant making abilities if you eat more salad.

But there's only two Super-Kids who even have that ability.

One makes massive Venus fly traps, and the other one . . .

Tyler Svec

I'm not sure what the other one does. Either way! If there's a day I'm going to choose to be hungry, it's that day.

You are required to eat all your food before you can leave the cafeteria, which on salad day is basically torture. It didn't take me long to figure out that I could just crunch the food to be very itty-bitty and throw it away when no one was watching.

One person was watching and thought it was the coolest thing, this little shrunken head of broccoli. So every day I shrink something for her and she has an entire collection of crunched items on her windowsill.

They became so popular, I was able to make a pretty good side job crunching items for people, just for the fun of it. $5 per item. Now they've become their own little underground market. (Technically speaking doing that sort of things is against the rules.)

The one thing that almost got me in trouble was when I crunched a tack for a guy. I should have thought about what he was going to do with it, but I didn't.

Let's just say there was a lot of very colorful language from Mrs. Darvensur when it was placed on her seat . . .

I'm a little more careful now about what I shrink, but for $5? Step on up and we'll see what I can do.

Afterwards, we'll usually spend an hour with a private instructor whose specialty is usually the same as ours. So my instructor, of course, was a Cruncher.

His name was Larry.

You work with them, and then you take some Super-Hero physics class.

It should be mentioned that all the 'normal' buildings neutralize our Super-Powers.

I'm not sure why you needed to know that now, but I told you.

Crunch

There is some written work that goes on with Super-School, but it looks a little different from what you see at any other school. For example, if your Super-Power is an X-Ray, or thermal scanning ability, you have to take your written tests in a special room so you can't read what's on everyone's paper.

But let's be real, none of you want to hear about the boring paperwork we have to do in super-school.

You want to hear about the best class.

Super-Ball.

It's really the only class that any of us ever really care about, because its uses are so much more practical.

Within the school there are various divisions of us. Normally these are determined by our Super-Powers. So all the Crunchers are a division, all the Super-Strength people are a division.

Overall there are usually thirty different divisions within a typical school year.

Super-Ball is our stage of glory.

You compete in various challenges throughout the week, testing your super skills. At the end of the week the top two in each division compete in what's unofficially called the 'Super-Ball-Brawl.'

We add the 'brawl' because it's fun. There's no actual brawling that happens.

If you do brawl, you loose Super-Points.

Don't worry I'll explain . . .

This is really the hard thing about telling you about this stuff, because so much connects to each other that it's hard to know where to start.

Super-Points, here we go!

Within a division you can earn points by doing good, cool, or awesome super stuff. If you break the rules, play dirty or are disrespectful, you loose Super-Points. You can earn or loose these even in the normal everyday activities as well.

When you graduate, your Super-Point score qualifies you for certain jobs. If you're the number one Cruncher in your region, you'll get more super calls.

You earn a lot of Super-Points during the game though . . .

Super-Ball-Brawl brings the top two people from every division and puts them in a secure underground arena to face off against each other.

Two teams of thirty people.

Last one standing gets the most Super-Points and all the glory.

It's a form of dodge-ball, except that we can use our various Super-Powers in any way we see fit.

Oh, that balls' flying at my face!

Crunch.

That was a nice pinball you threw at me. Take that! Then you chuck it as hard as you can at the other persons face!

We all have to wear protective suits, which keep us from dying, but still allow us to get sufficiently knocked around and feel a significant amount of pain.

In my first match, I lasted twenty seconds.

One guy threw a ball at me, and he could enlarge the item to ten times its original size.

I panicked and got knocked out.

Woke up three hours later.

It was awesome.

We play in an arena, but the playing field has a shield over it so there is no danger to the spectators.

I think the stadium seats almost ten thousand people. Usually there are fifteen thousand in attendance though.

Crunch

They really need to get more seating . . .

But seriously with all the 'sports' in literature, this would put them all to shame.

Where's Harry Potter? I'd love to see him survive when I crunch his wand into smithereens! Or when someone sets his broomstick on fire.

'Abracadabra!' Pah!

More like I'm going to Abraca-crunch your butt!

I know there are some die hard fans who are like 'Oh, Quidditch is the best sport ever.'

It really isn't.

Quidditch is really the worst thought out sport in all of literature.

'We have this really nice green field that we're never going to touch.'

Is the field padded?

'Heck no! We're not going to touch it. If we do touch it, it means we've fallen off our brooms, and are likely going to die because of the tremendous fall we've had.'

Don't you wear any protective gear?

'Now you're just talking crazy! Why would we wear protective gear? It's not like we have those big bludger balls you're trying to hit people with, which probably knocked us off our broom in the first place. And even better yet! We're going to have no protection for spectators! A stupid little 'snitch' that is worth more points than anything and basically means you win the game if you catch it . . .'

You might as well just have the game called Snitch and let the Seekers go at it.

Put fifty Seekers in there. Then you'd have a show.

Moral of the story . . .

Super-Ball-Brawl is way better!

Chapter 4

Now we'll skip ahead to my ninth grade year. One of the best years of my life.

I was sitting on a bench enjoying the shade from a large oak tree at the center of the campus. I was casually reading one of my course books, "Advanced Crunching for Dummies".

It was stuff I already knew, but Larry told me to read it.

So I was reading it.

At this point I probably wasn't going to remember any of it. I had kind of zoned out after page 342.

There's nothing more annoying than having to read a book that has information that you already know, in order to pass a test that you could pass with flying colors if they would let you just demonstrate the answer, as opposed to take a written test.

How many infrastructural crunching points are in a car?

WHO CARES? Let me crunch a car and then I can count them!

Or better yet, I'll send you a picture.

Ugh.

Crunch

But the point is I read it, right?

As I was sitting there, thinking about literally nothing, my attention was diverted from my book when an unmarked black car pulled up.

I've always concluded that it was divine intervention that the black car pulled at that moment.

Snapped me out of my almost-falling-asleep-from-boredom daze.

Now, on the other hand, I know black cars might sound shady, because every government uses black cars.

For years I wondered why they used only black cars. Did they get a discount on the color? Was black the color no one wanted?

It always amuses me in old TV shows, the good guys have the flashiest cars and somehow are never discovered by the bad guys.

Try that one in real life!

Point taken though, black cars do blend into darkness better than a bright yellow car.

With that in mind, there are two types of unmarked black cars . . .

Good ones, and bad ones.

The good ones are often four door sedans. Fairly normal looking. Normally, only two people inside.

The bad kind, generally are hummers or SUV's, something big and intimidating. Generally they're followed by a dozen black helicopters and an invisible strike team.

This was a good unmarked black car.

Out stepped two very official looking people. You knew right away not to mess with these people. They wore the sunglasses, and although you couldn't see any weapons, you knew they must have something hidden in their suit jackets.

They were both built like they could snap you in half with their big toes if they wanted to.

Tyler Svec

One of them pulled a couple of suitcases from the trunk of the car. The other moved around and opened the door for the person in the backseat.

Out stepped the most beautiful person I had ever laid eyes on.

Almost six feet tall, long wavy dirty blond hair with a single strand of bright red hair coming down on the left side. She wore dark sunglasses, bright red lipstick, and a long flowery blue dress.

Her dress was a bit strange, as it had long sleeves and buttoned up to her neck.

In some ways she looked like she belonged in the 1800's.

I'm not sure how she was surviving in clothing like that. It had been pushing 150 degrees for the past month.

Obviously not 150 degrees, but you get the point.

Whatever the reasoning behind her wardrobe, I certainly didn't mind.

She was quickly flanked on either side by her body guards, and she was marched right past me into the main campus office, without saying a word. At the time I was the only one sitting outside, and she did glance my way for a moment, and I'm pretty sure behind those dark sunglasses she winked at me.

She denies it, but I'm quite sure of it.

When someone denies something while smiling from ear to ear, it's kind of hard to believe.

Whenever it comes up in conversation now she just smiles and says with as straight but flirtatious of a voice as she can, *'I would never just wink at a stranger.'*

Then what were you doing winking at me?

'I didn't!'

Obviously, I married her, but you need to know her story, in order to know our story moving forward, so here goes!

Crunch

It was three days until I caught sight of her again, and when I did, it was in the school cafeteria. She was sitting all by herself in a corner, dressed similarly to what she had been the first day, except this dress was a different color.

Intrigued and scared out of my mind, I approached her and asked if I could sit with her.

To my surprise she said yes.

I can't say that I remember too much about what was for lunch that day, if I ate, or what I ate, but I enjoyed sitting and getting to know something about this new student who had (so easily) captured my attention.

She was 15 and from Sydney, Australia, so naturally she had (and still does to this day) a very thick Aussie accent.

Side-note. I've never had a problem with understanding any kind of accents, but my father can't understand anyone if they have even the slightest, and I do mean slightest, accent. So for years he never really talked to her directly, because he had no idea what the heck she was saying.

Her name was—

Hang on.

Have you ever just marveled at accents? I have.

Especially the Aussie one.

The year before, I had actually petitioned the student council to get Australian taught as a foreign language.

Sadly the petition didn't get approved by the school board, but I did have 1200 signatures on it!

That is an accomplishment.

Her name was Amanda Washername, and she had just moved here from Australia.

As I've already told you she didn't have any known Super-Hero history in her family. Her parents were missionaries to . . . can't remember the place right now, but they were missionaries!

She 'claimed' to have been bitten by a 'Cordellian Spider Snake.' Yadda, Yadda, Yadda.

Sorry, I buy the *'Cordellian Spider Snake'* story as much as I buy the *'I didn't wink at you'* story.

She was intriguing in many ways, but the one of the most unusual things about her was her Super-Power.

Her Super-Power was brand new, which is why she had been escorted to the school all special like. She had undergone a lot of testing to find out just what her power was.

As it turns out, my wife is a 'Roaster'.

Sure, you think I'm joking, but that is what the official paper work says. It's got her name . . . and then her age . . . and then under category, it says 'Roaster'.

Her Super-Power is that she radiates heat. The trick of it is, she doesn't feel the heat she's radiating, but everyone else will. If you're wanting to interrogate someone and make them uncomfortable, just put her in the room, within five minutes they'll be sweating like a three legged dog chasing down a wild boar in a desert.

We certainly had some interesting times as we got to know each other with this Super-Power.

At the time there was no known existence of this ability. So we were literally flying blind and seeing what happened.

As a result, as far as the divisions for Super-Ball went. She was all by herself which means she played in every game on the weekends, all of which I happily attended if I didn't make it into the game that week.

She won several of them, just because she made everyone so uncomfortable. When you have a fire breather, intentionally not using his fire breathing, because he's already dying of heat . . .

Crunch

That's impressive.

Her official Super-Name is "Firecracker."

Oh, you want to know the story behind this name? Well, I'd be very happy to tell you!

It was New Year's Eve, and we were picking up some fireworks for the party that was being put on at the school.

It is important for you to know that the one side-affect to her Super-Power is that the amount of heat she radiates is in relation to how much skin she has covered. Hence her very heavy, long, dresses.

I've always thought they looked good on her.

Amanda says I'm biased.

To which I reply, 'Maybe I am, but I'm right!'

She can't argue that.

It can also be affected by what she eats . . . we had just had spicy nachos at the Taco Shop.

We had gotten 50% off because we finished the 'Barn Burner Challenge.'

It was one of those challenges where they bring out chips with dip on them, each one getting hotter and hotter. Eventually you have to sign a waiver because it's so hot! I had to bow out at that point.

Not the case for my Super-Roaster girlfriend.

She won the challenge without breaking a sweat. Got her name in the paper and was basically a celebrity whenever we went back. Which was often, because she likes Mexican food.

We probably should have realized that having so much spicy food would do bad things, but it didn't occur to us at all. We had stopped at one of those big tents to pick up some fireworks for a New Year's Eve party we were attending . . . when literally the whole thing went up in smoke.

All she did was pick up a pack of firecrackers and it ignited!

Tyler Svec

The entire tent of fireworks went up in a spectacular fashion.

Huge fireball, lots of explosions.

It happened to be dark when we were there, so it made it look a little better because the sky was filled with all the lovely colors of fireworks.

No one was hurt, and surprisingly the owner of the tent wasn't that upset. He said (quote) *'he had been losing money on it for quite a while and was glad that he got to enjoy the fireworks for a change.'*

So from that day on Amanda has been known as "Firecracker."

But let it be known! That the one place you DO NOT want to take her is to a pool! Take her to a lake or an ocean, a river even, but NOT A POOL!

First five minutes you'll be fine.

Ten minutes that water will be starting to feel rather hot.

By fifteen minutes you had better be out of that water because you will be burning up and begging the ice making Super-Heroes to freeze her.

We discovered this the hard way, and I did come out of it with some slight burns.

What's really funny is if she stays in a pool for 30 minutes the water begins to steam and the water level will drop drastically every minute after that.

So pools are out.

This Super-Power does make certain tasks difficult. Like cooking for example.

Pancakes are out of the question.

You will end up with the most perfect black discs.

The first and only time this happened I tried to get her to keep them. I thought it would be cool, for me to crunch them down and then we could use them as coasters.

Crunch

She didn't like that idea.

Things that cook fast are, for the most part, not a good idea. As such our kids have never eaten hot-dogs because even by pulling them out of the package they get cooked and burned within seconds. She's never been particularly good at cooking steaks but she makes a mean burger. She's really good at chili and soups, but she has to pay very close attention to how long it cooks.

Most of our meals can be cooked in three minutes.

For some things she'll even wear oven gloves the entire time. It's a funny sight but one I've come to love.

Thanksgiving has always looked a little different for us. Normally for Thanksgiving we have turkey burgers, because the one thing that has been a disaster every single time we've tried to cook it, is a turkey!

It ends up so dry, it's like eating twice baked spaghetti where the noodles are made out of leather.

We definitely ate a lot of burnt suppers our first year of marriage.

You know what? Here's a little free marital advice: maybe you don't have a wife with this Super-Power, but no doubt there are things that don't turn out the way she wanted . . . just eat it.

Don't complain! Don't ask questions. Don't say *'This isn't how my mother made it!'*

Don't make a big deal if it's burnt, it's all going the same place regardless whether it tastes good going down or not.

Eat whatever is put in front of you and don't ask questions. Compliment the cook every time.

For the most part, our dating days found us spending lots of time walking through the woods and playing cards rather than going out on expensive dates. We didn't date right away and for a while we didn't even think about dating. We were just having fun together. We can remember a lot of times those first two years where we were by ourselves having fun, even though we weren't 'technically' dating.

I've come to think that it's best this way. We did fall in love, eventually, but it was slow and we got to know each other's character and see what was really important, rather than what usually is on the surface. We ate our supper together every night at the cafeteria and we attended a local church every week.

Only a few of us from the school attended church, but we have many good friends and memories that go along with it.

Now that we live in a more northern part of the world, where we get snow and stuff like that, it's a handy Super-Power. To this day we've never had to start a fire or light a furnace.

We save a ton of money, let me tell you.

Also, if you want your coffee reheated, let her hold it for 9 seconds and it'll be perfect.

10 seconds you'll be burning your mouth off.

11 seconds and you'd better not touch that coffee for at least a half hour.

Besides Amanda, there is only one other person who's known to have this Super-Power and that's our daughter, Victoria.

Needless to say, having two people with this Super-Power makes life even more interesting.

One time we took a family vacation. Victoria was probably six at the time, and we stayed at this hotel, and the pool was open 24 hours. We got the kids up and went swimming at 2 am in the morning, (Because no one else would be there.) We thought that with a bigger pool it would be good for us because it wouldn't heat up as quickly.

That's when we discovered that Victoria had the same ability. Once we figured it out Amanda and Victoria sat in the very hot, hot tub, while the rest of us went swimming. After an hour they had to get out because the water level had dropped to half.

Crunch

Victoria was once invited to go ice fishing with some friends from school . . .

I'm sure you can figure out how that went.

Now despite all the things that the two of them might struggle with, S'mores are great fun for all of us.

Once every summer we hold a contest to see if Amanda and Victoria can build *and* eat a S'more before it gets burned.

With as fast as they have to eat it, they end up looking like a S'more.

We must strike some people as strange because it can be the middle of the winter, -20 below zero, and we have two windows open, with Amanda and Victoria sitting in the living room drinking ice cold sweet tea with shorts and tank-tops on.

Our friends are so confused.

They come over and are like *'Oh, my goodness! How is it so hot in here?'*

I just point at Amanda. She makes a funny face, and our friends laugh. Life moves on.

Basically what it comes down to is, she's hot.

And yes, that's actually a true statement.

Chapter 5

At the beginning of this book I told you I had a weird life, and you're about to find out why I said that.

It was our senior year of high-school, and it was time for the Prom.

For the record, I actually hate dances. It involves small talk (which I don't particularly like), social expectations, and music that I don't like.

I've always been a fan of country music, not this hip-hop stuff.

Good country music that is, like from the 80's and 90's. And the early 2000's.

Amanda's always liked a bunch of Australian artists I've never heard of. Her go-to though is classical music. Beethoven, Bach and all those people. I have nothing against the classical music world; I actually do enjoy it.

It's a whole lot better than the hip-hop stuff.

I've tried to convince her that movie soundtracks count as classical music.

She doesn't totally agree or disagree with that statement, but when we got married she probably never thought that she would be

Crunch

woken up at 6 in the morning by her husband and seven kids jamming out to the Star Wars soundtrack . . .

So, basically I was talking about Prom.

Prom at Super-Schools is a bit of a circus, because not only do all the students, teachers, faculty attend, but parents and family member are invited to attend, too. The prom is kind of the pre-celebration for graduation, which happens the same weekend, and the kick-start to the summer.

The entire campus turns into one big concert/dance festival.

If you don't go, you are the weirdest person on the face of the earth, and you had better not be late . . .

We were late.

Amanda had been off-campus at her friend's house (her name was Amy), where I was supposed to pick her up for the dance.

I showed up looking reasonably well.

I don't wear ties. Or suit jackets.

So I looked good, but I didn't look like any James Bond.

I've never actually seen any James Bond movies.

I was running about a half hour early, and when I got there, I saw my (at the time) girlfriend Amanda, Amy and her family frantically running around the backyard. As it turned out, Amy's family raised sheep, and they had all escaped and were happily bounding around the property.

Now when I say sheep, I mean like 50 sheep.

They raised them for meat.

Tasted good, too. Just like chicken.

Except better than chicken, because chickens are as dumb as rocks.

Maybe they were smart at one point in time, but they've had their brains bred right out of them . . .

Tyler Svec

So you have 50 very fast sheep running around the property that (due to getting four inches of rain in two days) is very, very soggy. To make it even funnier, Amy's five sisters and all the boyfriends (who would be accompanying them to the dance) were present for this catch-the-escaped-sheep game. All together, there were probably fourteen of us, counting myself.

We were dressed in our nicest dance attire, gowns, dresses, tuxes —the works.

To catch sheep.

If you've never had the thrill of catching sheep, I'll give you a few highlights.

They can run very fast!

You end up feeling like Wylie-Coyote and the Road Runner, because the Road Runner keeps on winning, no matter what you do.

They can also jump very high. Just because you think you have them blocked . . . doesn't mean anything.

Next thing you know there's a 200 lb. animal flying through the air at you.

Good thing is, because they have so much wool, they are very soft when they hit you and it feels, really, like a pillow fight.

The property was also probably ten acres, so they had space to run.

To our credit we did catch every single sheep!

However by the end, we looked like we had been through five wars and had been attacked by mud-monsters.

The next hour and a half, consisted of a continuous line for the showers as well as a quick, but thorough washing off all our fancy clothes. The big blessing was Amy was what's called a 'squeegee,' so she can influence water particles, and therefore, both instantly soak something in water, or ring water out of an object with amazing proficiency. The clothes won't be completely dry when she is done with them, but once she is and you throw them in the dryer for twenty minutes, you're good to go.

All the visitors were kindly lent any clothes that would reasonably fit us while Amy was busy with all the laundry and the rest of the time was spent playing cards and having a good time. Really it was more fun than the prom ever would have been.

An hour later we were all dressed and looking good again.

A half hour after that, all the girls were actually ready.

Another piece of free advice, no matter how late you may be, enjoy it.

There are times I've wondered to myself which will be ready first, Amanda or the second coming of Christ. But no matter how much I wait . . .

It's always worth it.

I've never grown tired of waiting for her these 22 years.

When finally we were ready, we loaded up in our cars and took off to the school.

The next events almost made me think that it was some kind of Divine intervention, trying to keep us from getting to the dance. I hit every single red light, and I swear that they were longer than usual.

No one else in our company hit a red light. Only me!

Then just to top it off, a mere ten miles from the school, I had a flat tire.

So we changed the tire . . .

Now we were almost two hours later for the Prom, and we were both considering just not going. But still we decided that we should go, especially considering all the crazy things that had happened in the afternoon.

It was more like a celebration of, 'Yeehaw! We made it in one piece! We're alive!'

We stepped out of my car and took a big old breath of satisfaction.

With a smile and a nod from Amanda I took her by the hand and we walked into the school.

Now if I had been older and wiser or had been paying attention to anything other than my beautiful date, there are some things about that walk through the parking lot that should've caught my attention.

In retrospect, I should have seen the abnormally large Hummer in the back corner of the parking lot. It was all white, and the grill of the truck was pitch black and nearly three times the size of the ordinary grill.

Though I did note these things and think they were a bit strange, neither of us gave it any notice.

If we had, we might not have gone in.

And then we go back to that whole divine intervention thing . . . we were supposed to arrive right when we did.

We didn't know there was a problem until we came to Bart, who looked just as he always did on appearance. We happily announced ourselves at the entrance to the Super-School, and waited awkwardly for the whole, *'Have fun, you two, but not too much fun! And when you come back bring some of that good food I smell cooking.'*

Usually we always tried to bring him a plate full of the deserts, which are always superb.

Instead we got a cold shrug of a shoulder and he just stared off into space. Intrigued, we asked if something was wrong. To which he said,

'Get outta here, kids, I'm having a bad night.'

We were both taken aback, but to me something didn't sound quite right. Amanda caught it, too, and gently put her hand on my arm to get my attention.

Crunch

'Honey, I just realized I forgot my purse in your car,' Amanda had said to me. I knew right away what she was thinking. I walked between her and Bart, pretending to take her hand. Instead, as soon as I was clear Amanda had swung her purse at a Bart, who was suspiciously watching me, and not her.

It's long been my theory that woman have so many things stuffed in their purses that it feels like they have bricks in them . . .

Well she actually had a brick in it.

I always wondered why she carried it with her.

I guess we know why.

I'm just glad I wasn't Bart.

She clocked him upside the head, and he fell to the ground and was unconscious. Then our suspicions were proved to be true. As if a mask had been turned off we were looking at someone who was definitely not Bart.

Quick as we could, we pulled the unconscious man into the broom closet and closed the door. Next we heard a muffled yelling and after several minutes of following the yelling we realized it was coming from a red sedan near the entrance to the school.

The doors were locked and clearly whoever it was, was stuffed in the trunk. Quick as a flash I crunched the lock on the trunk and it popped open. Inside lay a tied and gagged Bart.

We hastily untied him and he let a big smile spread across his face. 'I thought I told you not to have too much fun,' he jovially remarked. Together we went back into the school and found the guy Amanda had knocked out (still sleeping like a baby) and searched him as Bart told us to. Eventually we found what we were looking for . . .

A card.

Now you should know that Super-Villains are an interesting bunch. While some parts of their society are very advanced with the latest research and technology, some aren't.

It's like within the Super-Villain society, there are the advanced ones and then there's the (as they call them) 'True Super-Villains'. The difference is the True Super-Villains don't use the new advanced technology.

Because they don't need it.

Because they're that much more evil.

So their theory goes.

What we had here, was a henchman of a "True Super-Villain".

We know that because it actually said Henchman on his Villain card...

It's kind of like ID in the Villain world.

Really bad idea. Talk about a security risk.

Stupid choice or not, it was helpful to know that we hadn't defeated the bad guy.

It also had his Super-boss's insignia on it. The sight of which sent chills up and down our spines.

An elaborate handle bar mustache.

We all tried to catch our breath. We had just caught a henchman of one of the most infamous Super-Villains of all time.

Mustachio!

It took a minute for that to really sink in, because Mustachio was the worst of the worst, and was known by one prominent feature. He himself wore a very large, very elaborate, very impressive handle bar mustache.

That's when we realized that the white hummer with over-sized grill must certainly be his. I could see now that the grill was meant to look like a mustache!

Immediately we knew that everyone below must certainly be in danger! I nodded to Amanda who instantly understood, and Bart

Crunch

fetched his mop bucket, which turned into a dark blue suit of armor, similar in looks to Iron Man.

Bart was always a fan of Iron Man, so it only made sense.

Within seconds he had transformed several of his mops into their various weapons and then strapped a couple of more on his back.

He was ready.

Amanda and I didn't have super suits. But that didn't stop Amanda from quickly removing the sleeves and four or five buttons from the top of her dress, in order to let more heat radiate so she could use it. She also was quickly plowing through a bag of jalapeno peppers she always kept in her purse, to enhance her Super-Power.

By this point she had gotten good enough she could harness the heat she radiated and set something on fire or make it hot if she wanted to, even if it was on the other side of the room. The catch was she had to see it.

Meanwhile, I feel totally lame because I don't have to get ready for anything because I just crunch items. The three of us stood, feeling nervous but knowing that it would be up to us to find Mustachio and catch him. Bart entered the secret password but it wouldn't work, no matter how many times he tried.

Finally, in a fit of frustration, he pulled out the mop with the electricity and overloaded the system with 20,000 volts of electricity.

The lock on the door popped open and we were in.

We had no sooner opened the door when 23 men (presumably henchman) came running into the building. Bart pushed us through the door and then closed it before we could get a word in edgewise. Amanda and I rushed down the hall, still able to hear music playing loudly.

We walked into the party which was alive and well. We were greeted by all our friends and as politely as we could we kept away from talking to anyone. We spotted my parents and ducked out of the way, performing a similar move when we spotted her parents who had flown from Australia. We had a mission, and it was to find Mustachio before he could cause any trouble or harm to people.

Just then, the music screeched awfully and then went dead, interrupted by a strange voice that was garbled but ultimately filled with the dreaded voice that far too many people had heard . . . Mustachio.

Everyone watched in horror as a great spotlight turned on behind him. Everyone covered their eyes and then stared at the silhouette in front of them.

Mustachio was tall and slim and the only defining feature anyone had ever seen of him was a magnificent handle-bar mustache that was so large it was clearly visible even though he was only a silhouette. While everyone else was in shock and trying to process what was happening, Amanda and I made a be-line for the side of the stage.

We could see more people filing in from the outside, creating a perimeter around the stunned masses. Amanda and I didn't have to think to hard to figure out what they were going to do.

In record time, we made it to the side of the stage, and for the most part, no one seemed to be paying any attention to us.

From here we could see Mustachio for who he really was. He was dressed all in white suit, pants, and hat, making him look like a skinny Boss Hog with a mustache. He held in his hand a strange weapon that we had never seen before. It was light brown in color, probably three feet long and eighteen inches thick. On the end was a strange white cap that somehow looked intimidating.

'I'll take the guys on the perimeter. You take him!' Amanda had told me.

'We won't be able to see them once we're up there,' I told her.

Crunch

'We will once you crunch the light,' she said with a wink and a smile.

'You ready?' I asked.

'I'm ready. Those peppers have kicked in now. I better do something soon or else I'm going to explode,' she said with a smile.

Without speaking we rushed the stage, I extended my hand and as easily as snapping my fingers, crunched the spotlight into a crumpled pile of metal trash. Mustachio whirled around in surprise.

I was frozen for a moment as he leveled the weapon at me. I could see Amanda had already jumped into action standing on the stage and using her heat to make all the weapons of the henchman scorch their hands. They dropped them and cursed loudly.

Mustachio turned around, seeing his men falling to the ground. He grabbed Amanda by her dress and threw her at me. We crashed to the floor and he pointed the weapon at us. He smiled, and silently gloated, but he did it just a little to long.

I reached out my hand to crunch the weapon, and he pulled the trigger. As it was crunched a blinding flash of light filled the room.

That was the last thing we saw.

Chapter 6

When I woke up I was lying on what appeared to be a hospital bed. Amanda was two feet away on an identical one. Five minutes later she woke from her slumber. By then I knew we weren't in a hospital, even though that's what it was supposed to look like.

I say 'looked' like because on first glance it looked exactly like a hospital, and if you had seen it, it probably would've totally fooled you. There were a few subtle differences . . . for one, the walls were a different shade of white than is in a typical hospital and there was a large red stripe that bordered the ceiling.

The sight of that alone was enough to get our attention.

Also, the doors were 13 inches wider. The nurse who greeted us when we woke had one blue fingernail, while all the others were plain, and there was a gentle, but slight hum of a Dia-hibillitic-enduser.

I know you have no idea what that is, but that's okay.

It neutralizes Super-Powers.

If you had heard it, you would've thought that it was just the ventilation system that was running, but to anyone in the Super

Crunch

community . . . it's a sound you don't want to hear.

That combined with the red stripe bordering the ceiling means you're deep in the bowels of the H.H.H. and something really bad just happened.

H.H.H. stands for Humans Helping Heroes.

Another of those wonderful acronyms governments around the world are famous for.

So the governmental structure of the world goes like such....

1.   Government : the part everyone sees.
2.   Secret Service : the part everyone knows about even if they don't see anything.
3.   HHH : (Bridging the gap) overseeing Super-Hero interactions. (Blah, Blah, blah)
4.   Sanction : Government body of the Super-Hero world.
5.   Super-Heroes : All of us.

To my knowledge no one had ever actually interacted directly with the H.H.H. in twenty years.

At least that's the story.

I'm sure *someone* had interacted with them, because the agency name implies that they are involved.

And really the horror stories you hear as a kid of the H.H.H.?

Those have to come from somewhere, right?

As it turns out, there was a H.H.H. center six hours away from the Super-School.

It was not long after we woke up that five men in black suits came marching into the room. Amanda and I both looked at each other and thought, *'Oh, crap! We're going to die.'*

Thankfully we didn't die, but we were swiftly (with doctors

approval) led through the halls to a large meeting room. The table inside was a ridiculous size.

You could've put fifty people around it.

Instead there were only five.

One of them was Bart.

Bart, and four babysitters.

We were certainly glad to see a friendly face, but it became evident very soon that we were not allowed to speak to each other.

Like at all.

I tried.

It was a bad idea, I'll just leave it at that.

Anyway . . . we sat there for the better part of an hour in complete boredom. Amanda and I eventually began making funny faces at Bart, just to amuse ourselves and make time go faster.

Bart laughed. Even the scary black suited people must have been laughing behind their sunglasses, because none of them stopped us.

Bart eventually joined in on the face-making.

Then we decided to do it to the black-suited guys.

I could tell there was a couple of them that just wanted to smack us.

But the bigger point here is that they didn't.

Which is good, because they clearly weren't here to kill us.

Just when we thought we would run out of ways to amuse ourselves, a man (Mr. Gents) came walking into the room and all but three black suits (leaving one standing directly behind each of us) left the room immediately.

That's when we found out what had really happened . . .

I had heard of Mustachio, by reputation, as had everyone else, and there are some super villains that are so good that only high up people even know what he does, because no one wants anyone to know that

Crunch

they know something on something that no one else knows nothing about.

Clear as mud, right?

The Long and Short of it is that Mustachio had been a very busy man as of late. Having pulled off 15 attacks in the past 11 weeks.

Have you ever seen something bad, but you couldn't help but acknowledge that in some sort of twisted way it was a good genius thing that had been done . . . in a bad sort of way.

It's like the *Despicable Me* movies.

You really want to say, oh, what a good movie . . .

No. Good job on the writers part for making you like a Super-Villain!

Rant over.

I've seen that movie way too many times.

When you have Super-Kids, it's kind of hard *not* to watch it. They want to catch Gru and of course in the end he doesn't get caught. It's a little disappointing. (From a Super-Hero's point of view).

As the kids have gotten older, we are still watching that movie, and pick it apart for what could actually be possible and what is just ridiculous.

But ultimately, that's how it was with Mustachio. It is impressive *and* bad that he had pulled off so many attacks.

His power was one of the more unique ones and that's why he had been so hard to catch in all the years I had heard of his name. He was an 'Archeloator'.

Don't feel bad if you don't know what that means, because I didn't know until the guy at the head of the table told me. Mustachio's Super-Power is that if he wants to, he can turn people into any object that he wishes, and on top of it he can make it appear to be as old as he wants.

Do the math, and it equals the chance to make a lot of money really quickly.

It was suspected that he had been turning anyone he captured into historical artifacts and selling them on the black market. One look at his now-seized bank accounts told us that not only was it his game, but he was playing it really well.

He had like $2,341,001.89 in one account!

That's when that old country song pops in your head...

'How do you get that job? That's what I want to know. Where ever he went to school, that's where I wanna-'

Okay, enough of that.

Now Super Villains are not the smartest bunch in the word. That might seems strange to hear, but it's true! Especially when they're rich. Where as most Super Villains would have gone to the effort and expense to build their own weapon . . .

Mustachio had gotten lazy.

It was called an Eraser, and no one knows what it does.

We didn't even know what it did, and we were there.

The Eraser had been bought on V-Bay (the Villains' form of eBay) two months prior, and as far as anyone can tell was a perfectly useless weapon at the time of purchasing.

In all seriousness, you would be surprised at the kind of things that people try to sell on the perspective Hero/Villain eBay.

One time, I was *this close* to buying a boat-car.

It was a boat that someone had attached wheels onto, so they could drive it down the highway! Can you even imagine?

Amanda nixed that purchase.

So, whatever the Eraser was intended to do, we're pretty sure what actually happened was a malfunction that happened at the time of firing, due to my beginning to crunch the weapon and Amanda beginning to heat the weapon with her power. The effects of the misfire destroyed much of the building and made everyone turn into babies.

That's not a typo, that's what actually happened.

My parents, her parents, all our friends . . . babies. Little babies. *Infants.*

It's a complete mystery why Amanda and I, or Bart for that matter were not affected by this. The best theory is that we were in the act of trying to stop him, and so we were saved. Perhaps it was divine intervention, though no one from the government would ever agree with that assessment.

The other quirk about everyone being turned into babies, is that they were instantly scattered all over the world. The only way they were able to confirm one way or another (via DNA Testing) what had happened is because a few of them (including a professor named Mr. Dinglebumhynder and the Snake King himself) were found on the doorstep of a church near Istanbul, Turkey.

To make things even stranger, every Super-School in the world had been affected by this.

Essentially this made Amanda, Bart and I the last Super-Heroes on the face of the earth.

After that, we were taken to rooms at separate locations, assigned six guards to each room, and not allowed to speak to each other for another two days.

When finally we did see each other again it was in another meeting, to discuss the *'latest findings'*.

In short, it was not known in all of this chaos if what had happened to the Super-Heroes had happened to Super-Villains or not.

But amidst all of this, they had confirmed that the Eraser had survived the debacle.

It had fallen from the sky over a village in South America.

Tyler Svec

The next night it had mysteriously gone missing.

Further research into the making of the weapon itself proved both that the creator had a sense of humor and that Mustachio didn't take the time to read the instruction manual as it appeared the effects of the weapon would start to wear off within twenty years.

As much as that might sound like good news, it didn't give us any peaceful thoughts.

All of us realized that either the H.H.H. would hide us as the only surviving Super-Heroes, or they would have us executed, leaving no witnesses to what had happened.

After the meeting, the three of us were allowed to spend the afternoon together, which did our spirits a lot of good. Over the next week we spent a lot of time in the Bible and in prayer, as it was the only thing we could rely on.

The rest was out of our control.

When the week was over, we were again brought into a meeting room, this time the only one in the room was Mr. Gents. Even the bodyguards were left outside and the five sets of doors closed.

After all the meetings that had happened in the past week, under Mr. Gents guidance, he had been able to convince everyone involved to leave us alive, but hide us. In the morning we were to be flown out on three different flights to three different locations, with brand new Ids, social security numbers, birthdates, everything you would expect to be set up with if you were in the witness protection program (or something of the sort).

And we didn't get a say in any of it.

We were allowed to spend supper together, and for once in private, giving us a chance to say goodbye.

We didn't have any other choices, or options. From our meeting we knew that Mr. Gents had gone farther than he should've to make

Crunch

sure we got this opportunity. We had to go along with it or we feared we would be killed. The three of us prayed and promised to try and find each other someday.

We were taken to our separate rooms, and as I lay there trying to fall asleep, I knew that I couldn't do what was being asked of me . . .

At least not alone.

At 1:00 am in the morning, I decided to use one of the contingency plans that I had concocted. I knocked out the one guard who was outside my door, crunched his weapons beyond being used ever again, took his wallet, and the new ID I had been given, and left the building.

By now, we all knew where each other was being kept and thanks to the car assigned to the agent I had knocked out, I made quick work of making it to Amanda's complex. I scaled the side of the building and tapped on her window, a quick crunch of the security device on the window, disabled it, but didn't set off any alarms.

I grabbed her by the hand and kissed her and we both knew what we were going to do.

She escaped through the window with me and we took the agent's car and drove almost six hours to our pastor's house. Though groggy, alarmed and confused, he was more happy to see us alive than anything. He married us on the spot. We suspect he must have known something about Super-Heroes because he didn't ask any specific questions that a person might ask, as if he was intentionally trying not to.

After that, we drove to the airport and booked an international flight to Australia, praying we would be able to live happily ever after. Though neither of us reasonably thought that using a stolen ID and jumping on a long airplane ride would go unnoticed by authorities.

When we arrived in Sydney we were promptly pulled aside by

Tyler Svec

airport security and in walks Mr. Gents who was all by himself and to our surprise, was smiling.

'I like the left-hand rings.'

We had hastily grabbed anything that would work as a ring. Mine, for example, was a toy ring from a *Lord of The Rings* Risk game that I had carried with me for years. Amanda's was nothing more than a piece of yarn we had wrapped around her finger.

'I think these ones would be a little better!' he had said, in an instant a man walked in with trays of rings for us to choose from. Confused, but not alarmed, we picked two and slipped them on our fingers.

'I had hated the thought of separating you, but it was the best I could do. But know this . . . I'm proud of you! You're doing what's right and that's not always what's easy,' Gents had told us. *'I want to make this work. However, you still need to go into hiding and go by your new identities. What can I do for you? Anything.'*

With his assistance we were set up with a nice honeymoon vacation and a small tour of Australia. I don't think I've ever seen Amanda so happy.

A week later we met with him again regarding the other request we had made.

'It'll take some time,' Gents had said. *'Are you sure you want to do this?'*

Amanda and I exchanged a look, strengthening our resolve.

'Like you said, it's not the easy thing to do but it's the right thing to do,' Amanda replied. The reply seemed to go right to Gents heart and push away any doubts he had.

'Then I will do my best to make it happen, I can't promise anything. You understand that right?'

We both nodded and the next next morning Amanda and I were

Crunch

on our way to our new out-of-the-way town where we would build our new life together.

Interlochen, Michigan.

Chapter 7

Now to say there was a lot of learning and adjusting to do in that first year of marriage was an understatement. Not only were we barely eighteen and married, working two jobs and doing life together, but within the year we became parents to four bright eyed babies.

That's right. I said four. But it's not quite what you think.

You know that other favor Mr. Gents was looking into? This was the favor.

He had spent six months searching through all the files and information about any and all documented babies that had been found on the day following Mustachio's attack. He was specifically looking for our parents.

It had taken him a serious amount of time, but finally he had tracked them down. Six months after we were married Amanda's mother Kirra was brought to us. A month later my father, Nathan, was found and brought to us. Then five months after that Amanda's father, Ethan, and my mother Bailey were found and brought to us.

Now to go back to my earlier theory about the 'Super-Gene' being

Crunch

deep within the DNA of Amanda's parents . . . this might prove that theory.

If they didn't have the gene, then why would they have gotten changed into babies?

All that aside . . . we looked like the most scandalous family to ever walk the face of the earth.

There are certain things that people expect from young couples (especially newlyweds) . . . 'having' four children is not generally on that list.

Let's face it—having four babies is not really on anybody's list these days.

Unless you're Amish.

Remember earlier in the book when I said it probably would've been easier for us if we had been Amish . . .

This is what I was talking about.

At the very least people don't expect newlyweds to have four at one time.

Even I will admit it was a little crazy, but it was the right thing to do.

Free life advice for you. The right thing to do is not always the easiest thing to do.

So there we are, eighteen, married, with a mini van and four young infants who are our parents.

Not going to lie, it was a little mind boggling when you're sitting up with your wife at 3 a.m. in the morning feeding your baby girl . . . only to remember that this *is* your mother.

There are some times it's really cool to be your father's father, because you get to put them in timeout.

Haha! Take that dad!

But on the same token, when your three year old is screaming at

Tyler Svec

you and throwing a tantrum you're almost scared to put them in timeout because they *are* your parents. And they're Super-Kids.

Praise the Lord none of them gained their Super-Powers until they were at least six.

We did cringe when we had to punish them for something, cause you're always thinking 'I hope this kid doesn't turn into lead or something like that'.

Ever see *The Incredibles 2?*

You know, possessed little Jack-Jack?

They didn't make that stuff up.

Well, they made some of it up . . . anyway.

Grocery shopping was a bit of a freak show.

Needless to say people knew when we walked into a place.

Everyone else has one kid, or two kids, when here we come. Pushing two double strollers and each pulling a shopping cart besides.

You remember I said Super-Kids eat a ton of food especially when they're growing. Apparently it applies to babies as well.

It hits another level of *'Wow, kid, where do you put all of that?'* when your six month old baby eats a whole box of canned baby food in one sitting.

And I'm not even going to talk about the amount of diapers we went through.

So much poop.

Thankfully Mr. Gents was able to get us some funding to pay for the abnormal costs that arose from this situation.

To make it even harder, since we were the only Super-Heroes on the face of the earth we had to keep our powers a secret . . .

That's just a funny concept right there.

Try explaining it when your six year old father picks up your *actual* truck to get a toy that rolled underneath.

Crunch

Or your daughter who has x-ray vision and is analyzing every injury she sees. "Oh, daddy, that girl broke her femur in 10 places."

"Wonderful! Why did you have to say that so loudly?!"

Then the girl with the injury stares at you as if to say *'Who the heck are you crazy stalkers?!'*

You just walk away and move on.

So, here are our kids and their powers.

Kirra (Amanda's mother) has the ability of x-ray vision.

Kirra's very helpful because we can get to the doctor for a various injury and know exactly what is wrong. So as such, she kind of became our household doctor. *'Oh, man, did you just get smacked in the side by the basketball I crunched? Come here, Kirra!'*

In ten seconds or less, Kirra will know if there are any internal injuries. Rather handy.

Though the doctors are generally quite annoyed when you give your own diagnosis and happen to coincidentally be right.

Every time.

She isn't usually able to treat the injuries, but she can at least identify them.

Next there's Ethan (Amanda's father). His Super-Power is boxing.

I suppose you could call it Super-Punching.

If he got mad, look out!

He's basically like Wreck-it-Ralph. Except not huge and red.

He actually doesn't even like red.

He's a green person. Anyway . . .

If he even touched the wall with any amount of anger, you'd have a hole punched clear through the wall. Like, you could see clear into the next room in the house.

It did come in handy when we needed to take down this shed behind our house. We let him at it.

Tyler Svec

Five minutes later it was gone! Like it had never even been there! Wonderful power, really.

We once had to pay to replace an arcade game of wack-a-mole.

Let's just say, he got the mole.

Then there are times when you get frustrated with your TV, or some other small electronic device and you give it a tap . . .

So much for that TV.

And radio.

I probably shouldn't even mention the microwave . . .

Okay, I have to mention that, it's a great story.

So for a long time, I had wanted to blow up a microwave. So we decided to give it our best shot. We filled this thing with cans of gasoline and firecrackers and other explosive items. The idea being when I crunched it, it would just explode instantaneously.

I will admit, Amanda and Victoria weren't home, and for that matter Amanda didn't know about this. In retrospect, we should've just had the two of them eat some peppers and heat the stuff up.

I crunched it and . . . well, it didn't explode. Everything just was crunched and made smaller.

Then before any of us had a chance to use our brains in any reasonable way, Ethan gave the microwave a single frustrated smack on the top.

Boom. It exploded.

'Goodness, gracious, great balls of fire!'

Ethan and I got some pretty serious burns and concussions.

It worked out okay, because Nathan carried us to the car, Kirra diagnosed our injuries, then Nathan drove us to the hospital, and all was okay.

Though Amanda and Victoria did get a call from the emergency room in the middle of a Ladies' Bible Study.

Crunch

So there was that.

Not joking, but she was pretty steamed about it.

Now we can laugh, though.

That's one of the important things about any marriage—you just have to be able to laugh at stupid stuff that happens and move on.

Next we have my my father, Nathan. My dad, Nathan, has Super-Strength, which is not to be confused with Super-Punching because there is a difference. Super-Strength can lift stuff, but not punch.

Ethan can punch his way through anything, but is completely useless if you need him to lift anything heavy. Like, anything. We asked him once to help carry bags of feed from the truck to the barn. They're fifty pounds a piece. Couldn't lift a single one. He got frustrated at Nathan for teasing him and punched the bag . . .

Big mistake.

But if you need an appliance lifted, call Nathan. Got a flat tire and your jack isn't working? Call Nathan. He works in construction now, and is able to easily impress everyone with how much he can lift.

He was the only kid in weights and conditioning class to bench press fifteen hundred pounds.

After that we did have to tell him to tone it down just a little so we didn't get any attention.

It was hard to keep this secret under wraps when your six year old is pulling out trees in the yard to look for bugs in the dirt. Let's just say, our neighbors were pretty freaked.

Then there's my mother, Bailey who is (as we call it) an E.M.P.

Of course E.M.P. stands for Electromagnetic Pulse. You can fry just about any electrical device with one if you know what you're doing.

And when she's just learning about it, you end up frying a lot of things that . . . you didn't want fried. For several years Amanda and I just gave up on cell-phones because Bailey would touch it, and it would

Tyler Svec

be dead.

When we got to the dating years, her boyfriend at the time dumped her, so she fried the engine in his very expensive, tricked out 1971 mustang convertible. And by fried, I mean deep-fried with whip cream on top! There was no redeeming that engine.

I felt a little bad for the guy, but I hadn't liked him that much anyway.

He was totally opposed to John Deere tractors.

The way I see it, John Deere tractors are the best because of the color. Green.

It's God's color.

I know some of you are like UGH! But hear me out, for green to be such a bad color he sure put a lot of it on the earth. Trees, plants, crops.

Therefore, that makes John Deere tractors close to divine.

I know that's a bit of a stretch, but sometimes delusions are fun.

And, just in case we didn't look completely insane . . . Amanda and I were blessed with the birth of fraternal twins Mikayla and Brent two years after our parents came to us.

We love them both, they are both as different as night and day, and Mikayla has one of the weirdest Super-Powers that even made Mr. Gents shake his head.

Nothing would stick to her.

Stickers. Duct-tape. Glue. Spray foam. Nothing.

It made her literally the cleanest kid on the planet.

Her sweat didn't even stick to her like a normal person. It formed little beads and rolled right off of her as if she was covered in a layer of wax. She could stand out in a torrential down pour for twenty minutes and come out of it completely dry.

Her clothes would be soaked but her skin was as dry as anything.

Crunch

No dirt would stick to her.

We even had to buy special, dry shampoo for her because it was the only thing that would stay in her hair. Telling her to get a shower was almost useless because she never smelled bad. We made her get a shower just to keep it fair.

The girl also had a strange connection to spiders for whatever reason. Maybe it was because nothing would stick to her and the spiders liked it, but there was always—and I do mean always—51 spiders on the ceiling in her room.

No matter how hard we tried we could not get rid of them. We would go in there . . . crunch and roast them all into oblivion.

5 minutes later . . . they were all back.

We gave up.

Mikayla had them all named.

Her sisters refused to share a room with her because she always said in the middle of the night she would sick the spiders on all of them if they snored in the slightest.

The biggest irony of this is Mikayla snores like a brass band stuck in a cave.

But Brent is very different.

We call him the "Ice-man".

I know that some of you are groaning, but he literally makes everything cold.

It's like having the opposite power of Amanda and Victoria.

Victoria, if you remember, is our daughter with the same Super-Power as Amanda. She's the baby of the family. Born two years after the twins.

Just when people thought we were done having kids . . .

Haha, take that people!

But in all reality, God planned that one, not us. We were thrilled to

Tyler Svec

welcome another child into the world.

I have yet to figure out who lets off more heat—Victoria or Amanda.

It has been the source of many debates in the house, and so finally when Victoria was 12, we decided to create a test.

We'll just call it the Hot-Olympics.

I know it sounds weird, but what would you call it?

The "Hottest" contest?

The "Roaster Games"?

Whatever you want to call it we put on this little contest...

Three stages.

The final stage, (Which we called *Survivor*) included us putting *Mr. Ice Man* himself in our storage shed with the perspective contestants. Then we timed how long he lasted.

Victoria was the winner, as Brent only lasted 36 seconds before he came running out, screaming like a wild maniac.

With Amanda it took 38 seconds and she claims to this day it was an unfair match.

Her reasoning . . .

'Victoria's still too young to fully control her roasting ability.'

Yeah. Okay, we'll go with that.

Meanwhile, I'm trying not laugh.

But seriously when you get Brent, Amanda and Victoria together . . .

The combination of the three of them together can make winter the most dangerous time of the year.

They had to close the Crystal Mountain ski-resort once, because everything got too icy.

We pretended to be just as shocked as everyone else.

How did it get so icy!?

Crunch

Thankfully, we were not connected to that incident at all. That being said, the three of them do create awesome sledding tracks.

First you send Amanda and Victoria down the hill, then you send Brent.

The result is a path that turns to solid ice and can easily get you going up to 35 miles per hour on a regular plastic sled.

If you use a metal sled you should really have health insurance . . . because you're going to need it.

The first and only time I tried a metal sled, I got going WAY too fast! I had to crunch like 3 dozen trees so I didn't kill myself.

Our neighbors asked why we cut the trees down . . . we said they fell over in the windstorm that went through last night. They didn't believe us, but we just said, *'How did you not hear that? It was the worst wind storm I've ever been through.*

I think they bought it, but if not, oh well.

Just another example of the awkward situations that can arise from having Super-Kids. We were blessed to have a good, sizable amount of land that was partially forested, so we could play and have fun without being seen by too many people.

However, a fence was necessary when we put in a basketball hoop. Due to Mr. Super-Strength, Nathan (My father in case you forgot), we all had to wear pads, helmets,and gloves no matter what game we were playing. Depending on who had it last it could be super hot, super cold, or come at you like a wrecking ball . . .

We had a couple of balls explode on us because even with the gloves, Amanda and Victoria would accidentally heat it up too much.

Bang.

Took us by surprise the first time. If Brent held it too long. You might as well be throwing a block of ice at a person.

'Do you want to build a snowman?'

Tyler Svec

I would love to, but you're going to turn it into ice as soon as you touch it, *Mr. Ice-man!*'

So there you are, complete insanity. It took some adjusting, to say the least.

We never told anyone else the truth about the fact that we were raising our parents. We just simply told them that we had always wanted to adopt.

Besides, they wouldn't have believed us even if we had told them.

Just as a side-note: for whatever reason, our parents ended up having different Super-Powers then they had previously. For one thing, Amanda's parents hadn't had any Super-Powers until we were raising them, and my parents had changed. My dad (Nathan) was originally a Shape-Shifter and my mother, (Bailey) was a plant grower.

She could grow anything and never had to water it. Our garden growing up always looked fantastic, because she could even control which plants she grew and which ones she made wither.

As much as raising seven Super-Kids made for some awkward situations, there are far more good or funny memories from that time in life.

In all seriousness though, even though other people freaked out and treated us like we were some kind of diseased species, we actually loved it, and for the most part we didn't find it awkward that we were raising our parents. Most of the time we actually forgot about it altogether.

Chapter 8

Overall, the small little town of Interlochen proved to be one of the best places for us. Not only was the community small, but it did have everything that we needed without always having to drive all the way into town. Because no matter how hard we tried, we always attracted a certain amount of attention . . .

It probably didn't help us out any that we had by now gotten a large 12 passenger van and had painted it blue because Amanda couldn't stand the color white for whatever reason. So we were, in a sense, very noticeable when we were pulling into town.

I had wanted to paint it like the A-Team.

That would've been awesome.

But blue it was!

Within reasonable walking distance of our house there was a library, a restaurant, a state park, a descent grocery store, ice cream shop, and a mini-golf course.

Though, we had to be pretty careful when we went to the mini-golf course

Tyler Svec

Lets face it—you have a mini-golf course and nine people with Super-Powers—something's bound to happen.

You should have seen the size of that golf ball when I crunched it. It was so tiny.

Looked like a marble.

The only problem was, after that I couldn't un-crunch it so I was stuck smacking around this little marble for the rest of the game.

I kept it though. Sits on the mantle at our house.

We found a good church and for many years lived as good and peaceful of a life as we could. Mr. Gents, whose real name we found out was Gene, strangely became our good friend in ways that we always felt was unusual for a government agent. He must have liked us because he stuck around. Eventually, he even bought a house and moved in just a few doors down from us.

From that point on he came over to dinner every Friday night and we would play games. And after a while he even showed up at church, much to our surprise.

As the years passed, bits and pieces of what had gone down at the H.H.H. came to light. It turned out that while everyone else had wanted to 'finish' us off that week, we had been held by the H.H.H. Gene had single-handily stuck up for us and fought to leave us alive and had struck a deal with them.

He had been allowed to help us, but he was forced to resign and was never allowed to work for the government again.

That being said, if he needed to research anything we asked of him or needed assistance, he still had a number of friends who would look it up for him . . . off the books, so to speak.

Now, out of all of the things that I could've been prepared for . . . there was one thing I had never seen coming.

Amanda and the kids wanted to get a pet.

73

Crunch

I was not huge on pets; for one thing I felt like it could be hazardous to the animal, if any of our powers should get out of control . . .

We tried goldfish first.

Talk about a short life.

One got deep fried when Victoria touched it. The next joined the frozen food division when Brent had reached in the bowl. Bailey electrocuted a fish to smithereens.

There's cooking the fish, and then there's what Bailey did to it.

It was bad.

Funny, but bad.

But never to worry, after each one Kirra so generously provided all the crucial details about what was broken in the fish, specifics on how it died and the agony the fish had gone through.

After all of that, there was only one fish left. So I waited until it swam through the little castle and then . . .

"Crunch!" The castle was now the size of a golf ball!

Oops! How did that happen?

That too has joined my collection of things on the mantel.

I felt a little bad about it later.

But the kids were very much in awe at how I had crunched it and Kirra was a little too eager to tell of all the injuries the fish had sustained.

She also told her friends at school.

Just another example of your kids putting you in awkward situations.

As a side-note: Captain Crunch was their favorite cereal when they were little.

I still like it . . . it's like they made it just for me! The box is even yellow like my super-suit.

Tyler Svec

But back to the point . . . I was hesitant to get a pet.

By this point, our four oldest kids were ten and overall they were improving on controlling their powers, and so I said we could get a cat . . .

Figured nine lives would help things out a bit.

So we began the search for our family cat.

We ended up going about ten miles to a family farm (owned by some people named Svec) that had some barn cats up for grabs.

The kids looked at all the cute little fluffy things and then picked out the kitten they wanted . . .

Then they asked the cat's name.

That's when post-traumatic stress kicked in for me.

The kitten's name was Mustachio!

I heard that name, and it was all I could do to keep from crunching that cat right there!

To be fair, the name was fitting, because he was a mostly white cat, with a black bit of fur over his top lip to make it look like a mustache! (there's even a picture in the back of the book)

I tried really hard to talk the kids into another kitten . . . but no, Mustachio it was.

As we were deciding which cat to choose I couldn't help but wonder if the Svec's actually knew who Mustachio was? Surely his name had inspired them to choose that name for their cat . . .

But no, it turns out he just looked like he had a mustache.

So we took him home.

I really wished I had been able to convince the kids to name him something different, but to no avail.

Therefore, Mustachio was our house cat for a very long time.

Unfortunately, in some ways he was a very likable cat. He was also a very stupid cat.

Crunch

Ironically, that cat is still alive . . .

Despite the cat, we became good friends with the Svec's, who seemed to not notice that we had seven kids. At least not notice in the good way where you could tell they weren't going to make bad comments about you behind your back . . . or to your face.

They had ducks. Happiest creatures you have ever seen.

If they had been huge fans of chickens I probably would've reconsidered being friends with them . . . because chickens are stupid.

Na, I'm just kidding.

Well, I'm not kidding about the chickens being stupid.

And to make it even better the Svec's had a meat store where we could buy as much meat as we wanted.

Which is good, because as I told you earlier, meat is essential to a Super-Hero's diet.

It had good prices, too. Saved us a lot of money.

So one Saturday morning I was heading over to their meat store when something unexpected happened. I had just pulled into the meat store and was getting out of our large van when a fair sized blue SUV pulled up next to us.

The fact that it was blue should've gotten my attention.

Next thing I know, Bart steps out and is giving me probably the biggest hug I've ever had, all the while smiling from ear to ear.

It took me a minute to process what had just happened, but after that I was thrilled, too.

Supper that evening was the best reunion any of us could have asked for. We invited Gene over and Bart and his family. He'd been married a year or two ago and had a little one of his own and now lived just a few miles away in Buckley.

Turns out Gene hadn't been allowed to know exactly where Bart had been sent, but he knew he had been sent to Northern Michigan somewhere. That was why he had placed us in Interlochen, hoping we would all meet again someday.

As you can imagine we became very good friends over the next few years and saw each other often. Late at night when the kids were in bed, we did have several discussions among us adults about what would happen if and when the effects of the Eraser would wear off. Would our parents remember everything? Would the real Mustachio already be strong and powerful? Did anyone know where Mustachio even was?

Gene promised to look into all our questions from some of his still friendly connections in the government, but ultimately he came up empty. It seemed as if the entire government had entirely forgotten about the existence of Super-Heroes.

Even that possibility made us suspicious.

Did they actually forget? Or was this a sadistic part of Mustachio's greater plan?

For the moment we didn't know, we would just have to wait and see.

Years passed and life went on as all of us became like family to each other.

However, one other thing that had been haunting me ever since we had adopted our parents was what would happen when puberty hit.

Lord help us all.

Not only were we faced with the prospect of having seven teenage kids at once, Amanda and I were uniquely faced with the awkward reality of having to tell our *parents* about the birds and the bees and everything that goes along with that . . .

It doesn't really get more awkward than that. Let me tell you.

Literally, you're sitting there telling your parents how babies are

Crunch

made, and you *are* the baby!

As you can imagine when you are in such a conversation, there are some strange thoughts that go through ones mind . . .

For example: If you have never heard the Ray Steven's song, "I'm My Own Grandpa," go and look it up and then you will understand.

I'm my father's son, but now I'm also my father's father. Which indirectly makes me my own grandpa.

Let alone when my father should get married . . . his son would both be my half-brother and my grandson?

And then, if my mother got married to someone else . . . and she had a child. I would also be a half-brother/ he would be my grandson / and he would be my step father?

To make things even weirder and stranger, Amanda and I soon realized that if our parents truly don't have any memories of their life prior . . . they might want to date other people.

Should we allow that?

Due to the fact that our parents have no memories that we are their kids, if we didn't allow them to date other people, we would be the worst parents on the face of the earth. At the same time you're having a conversation with your father, about dating this girl from church, and all you really want to do is yell out:

'YOU'RE SUPPOSED TO MARRY YOUR SISTER!'

Which sounds bad on so many other levels.

But technically speaking, because none of the kids are truly genetically related, our kids could marry our parents or they could marry almost any combination they wanted and be totally fine . . .

Do you see the agony we went through?

Then when your mother gets asked out by this guy from school, and you're trying to be nice and friendly to the guy, but you're hurting inside . . .

Tyler Svec

We insisted on meeting whoever our kids wanted to go out with.
I tried to be as polite, but intimidating as I could.
Didn't want any of them getting ideas of any kind.
So while we're sitting there, those lines that fathers are famous for are going through my head . . .
"You so much as even touch my daughter/mother/mother-in-law and I will crunch you so hard you'll be kissing your butt for the next twenty years!"
I thought of getting a gun, for the sole purpose of 'cleaning the gun' when they came to pick up our daughters.
Scare the crap out of the kid from the get-go, and there won't be any problems. Right?
Amanda was a little better at being civil about it. In the end we allowed them to date other people, because they didn't know about their own past in that way.
Thankfully, none of those relationships stayed together for more than a year.
But, you talk about a stressful time in life? That one takes the cake.

Chapter 9

Our nerves began to get the better of us to some extent, the closer and closer we got to our parents turning that magical age of twenty. If everything we knew about the Eraser could be believed, by the age of twenty our parents would remember everything . . . but nothing said it wouldn't happen when they were younger.

At some point the effects of the Eraser would begin to wear off.

Gene kept in touch with all of his still friendly contacts, and we kept all our ears and eyes open as we searched for any sign of Mustachio.

Every week we had a meeting between him, our family, and Bart, and even the Svec's were allowed to join the meetings as they had by now become trusted friends of ours.

Life went on, and the mythical year grew ever closer.

Amidst all that life brought our way nothing, and I do mean nothing, could have prepared us for a sophomore Mikayla and her prospective senior boyfriend.

As you might imagine, Amanda and I were a little uneasy about this, but nonetheless, Mikayla had taken a particular liking to a senior

Tyler Svec

from Buckley named Miles Winkle.

As is custom before every one of our kids starts dating anyone, we have to meet their date several times, and so he was to join us for a dinner one Saturday night.

I just about had a heart attack when I saw the kid.

He was tall and slim, with a white Stetson cowboy hat on his head. I approved of the hat.

But he had a very similar appearance to that haunting memory of Mustachio.

He even had the starts of a mustache on his upper lip, and he had driven up in a white Prius.

Mikayla rushed to the door before either of us could get there and politely invited him in.

Now we could see that he was dressed all in white, completing the image of Mustachio.

Amanda noticed my alarm and clearly was hiding her own alarm. Then we noticed something that we hadn't expected . . .

He seemed nervous.

Confused by this, Amanda and I managed to make it through the night without having a heart attack. As we sat there at dinner with the entire family and got to know Miles Winkle at least a little bit, I couldn't help but notice two things . . .

Mikayla and Miles were head over heels for each other, and he seemed to be a very reasonable and polite young man.

To say we were confused and thrown off by this innocent demeanor was an understatement. Was this part of his plan and *was* this even the great Mustachio? Or were our imaginations getting the better of us?

Strangely, and to our great surprise, the alarms seemed to get quieter as the night went on.

Crunch

As if we weren't confused enough, our cat (named Mustachio) seemed to be in love with him. Miles happily petted the cat and was amused at its name.

He even asked where we came up with the name.

'He came with it,' I had said.

Immediately after he left for the night, I picked up the phone and frantically arranged for everyone involved to come over the next night to discuss the new happenings.

To say the others were surprised was a bit of an understatement, too, and I'm not sure if we truly came to any kind of conclusion. A few calls later and Gene was able to get all the records on Miles Winkle. According to all of Gene's sources he had indeed been adopted, though the records were fuzzy on where exactly he had been found or the circumstances.

As far as official sources were concerned, he was a senior at Buckley, top of his class. Bart (whose kids also went to Buckley) had only heard good things about the kid, and as it turns out everyone attended the same youth group which is where Mikayla and Miles had met each other.

So while we were unsure of what to do, Miles and Mikayla and their relationship continued to grow. The more I was around him, the more I began to not fear him at all. In fact he turned out to be a very nice young man.

That being said, in the back of my mind I was always waiting for him to slip up in his act (if it was an act) and spill a hint or something that might indicate that he was acting.

But in three months time, there was no slip. Not even a hint of one. We were baffled, and by the time Christmas rolled around, we were nearly all convinced that Miles Winkle was who he said he was.

As much as I didn't want to I begin to think of him like family, he came to church with us and proved to have character that went far beyond what we had first expected.

Finally one day our lucky break came. We found a single hair of his laying on the kitchen table after he had left. A few phone calls and lab tests later and it turned out that the DNA collected from the hair was a perfect match for Mustachio.

By now, all of us involved were entirely unsure what to do.

Try as hard as I could, I could hardly dish up any distaste or disapproval for Miles Winkle. The DNA may have been a perfect match for Mustachio but nothing else added up. He still, apparently, had an unusual affinity for the color white.

He even donned his white suit for church every Sunday.

But aside from that he seemed to be completely normal.

It was only two months after that, when Mikayla, Miles and I were sitting around a campfire late one Friday night that they clearly had something to ask me.

'Mr. Braymend, I have something to ask you,' Miles had said.

Having no idea what was coming, I prepared for what I thought might be asked as Mikayla gently but loving nudged him in the side. He hesitated as if unsure, but seemed to drum up the courage to say something he must have been thinking for a long time. Surprisingly I found myself saying . . .

'You can ask me anything. You know that.'

I'm not sure where that came from, but something had come over me, only in retrospect do I see that God's hand was on me at that moment.

He proceeded to share with me his Super-Power, but he had no idea what it was or what to do with it. He looked scared and finally it became clear that Mikayla had said that I would be able to help him.

Unsure of what to do at that moment, I promised to help him, and

Crunch

he did a slight demonstration of his power, by turning my coffee mug into a goblet, that later we learned, looked like it was from the sixth century.

It's worth a lot of money, but I keep it on our mantle now.

As you can imagine, this threw all of us for a big loop. Bart, Gene, and everyone else involved sat up way to late one night talking and discussing the phenomenon before us.

Here was Mustachio. Once the greatest Super-Villain to ever live . . . now he was a teenage boy who didn't even know anything about Super-Heroes.

The implications were confusing.

The biggest unknown question was: Would his memories return like everyone else's were supposed to? So far the answer was no.

We had begun to notice in our four oldest kids (who were our parents) that they seemed to be changing, and Amanda and I were quite certain they were beginning to have some awakening inside their minds. It was subtle and would have gone unnoticed by everyone else. But there *was* something on the horizon.

Gene called his contacts and got all the information he could on the issue. It was said that perhaps because Mustachio had been the one closest to the Eraser, that the effects would be greater on him . . . maybe even permanent.

What would happen if he never remembered anything?

For now that seemed to be the case and while Gene looked into one other thing we knew we would all have to do.

We took Miles under our wing, and collectively we informed him that we were Super-Heroes, too. The look on his face was hilarious when he finally learned of our Super-Powers.

From that point on he became a truly unofficial member of his family, and we became well acquainted with his family. They were allowed to know the secrets, and they were very relieved having not known what to do with their son's unique abilities.

Whether it was due to the effects of the Eraser or divine intervention, Miles had only just discovered his ability.

So naturally we were back into training someone on how to use a Super-Power.

By now I would say we were quite accustomed to it, and really it wasn't too hard.

Now you might be thinking that someone who can turn things into old objects can't be that hard to teach.

For the most part you're right, but there are still very dangerous moments when they can't yet control the Super-Power.

A game of football could turn deadly at any moment, where we had a number of footballs accidentally get changed into ancient bricks that were hurtling through the air.

Thankfully, there were never any injuries as everyone took it as a chance to react and 'save the day' by morphing the football in some way.

Amanda and Victoria could super heat the ball to explode.

Brent could turn it into a ball of ice.

Kirra and Mikayla couldn't really do anything to it.

Bailey could explode it with electricity.

Nathan and Ethan could both either punch or break it to smithereens.

And of course I could crunch it.

It was like an Olympic sport to see who 'saved the day' first.

Usually, it was me.

I also have one of those sitting on our mantle.

One time we were out at a restaurant, (which admittedly is a risk) and all of our napkins kept getting changed into doilies.

Crunch

But then, he changed all the useless coasters they give you at restaurants into perfectly ancient and beautiful tiles of amazing color.

If I ever had to think of this kid as a son-in-law I can only imagine at the amazing work of art Mikayla's ring would be.

Then there was the time, it was just he and I driving back from Home-Depot in my old beat-up pickup truck when I dared Miles to change it into something ancient.

That was a bad move as we soon found ourselves driving a Model-T that went about twenty miles per hour.

We did sell that car.

Then the funniest and most horrible thing that ever happened.

Once again, we were playing mini-golf and he accidentally changed his golf ball into the biggest, most beautiful diamond you've ever seen.

We all dove towards the hole like a bunch of Rugby players trying to get the ball.

Sadly, it turned out it was the eighteenth hole and the ball was gone.

Coincidentally, the golf course got a face lift the next year.

But as life went on, Amanda, Bart, Gene and I were busy behind the scenes, getting ready.

There was one thing we still had to do.

Chapter 10

With the discovery that Miles Winkle (Mustachio) was no longer a threat in the way we expected, we were besides ourselves with confusion at first.

We continued to watch carefully, but overall the only thing that Miles seemed to inflict was a sense that he had completely stolen Mikayla's heart and would one day likely become my son-in-law.

Strange as that would be.

Though by this time I kind of liked the guy.

Still, I was always wondering, if his memories returned, what would happen?

At this point I hated to mess up their relationship, and if Miles remembered that he was indeed Mustachio . . . would anything change?

Despite the uncertainties of what might lay before us, we all agreed on one thing . . . if Mustachio was not going to be a threat, than we had to at least make sure and destroy the weapon that had caused all of this.

For the moment, it meant a great deal of work for Gene, and not

Crunch

that much for us.

At least not right away. As I told you, the weapon had mysteriously disappeared a day after it had been found, and since then no one had cared about the weapon, it seemed.

For several months he searched and searched, but ultimately came up empty.

Then came our big break.

One of Gene's friends deep in the government had once had some connections with some family members who were less-than-upstanding citizens.

There was a chance that he would be able to figure out something.

A month later, he did have some information for us.

They had busted the person who had stolen the weapon, and as the report had said years ago, the weapon was not to be found.

The only lead that his friend could give us was the the criminal (Wyatt Dyrt) had a small cabin somewhere around Curtis Lake in the Upper Peninsula.

I wasn't quite sure where that was, but we looked it up on a map and decided that we had to at least give it a concerted effort to search the area over the course of the summer.

So all four of our oldest kids (our parents) graduated and the open houses and everything associated with graduating took place.

Then we changed our focus.

The kids by now had been brought into the loop, at least a little.

They still didn't know that they were our parents.

There was only so much we thought we could tell them without it getting weird.

So for now, searching for some super-secret bad guy weapon from our high-school days was good enough.

Tyler Svec

It took a bit of planning and several trips up to the area before we concluded that we had absolutely no idea what we were looking for.

We couldn't find his house.

Or public records of him.

He had gone to jail and hadn't even been released.

He had died several years into his sentence and was buried somewhere in Delaware.

We were hard pressed, to say the least.

The thing that changed our fortunes, (at least a little) was that the Svec's had been to Curtis Lake before.

Turns out they had taken a vacation there several years back and had done a bit of kayaking on Curtis lake. They explained that there were 3 islands in the middle of it. Two of them were untouched, while the third one had a small cabin on it.

Not much to look at, they had said.

It was also apparently seagull infested.

Thrilled to have new information, we were filled with certainty that this time we would find what we were looking for.

So we made our plans, in which we invited Miles to join us.

I know it seems like a weird move, but by this point he was basically family anyway.

How could we not?

He was excited to say the least.

The night before we were all to leave we met at Gene's house where he presented each of us with our very own Super-Suit. Normally you would get a Super-Suit when you graduated school, but by all technicalities Amanda and I had never officially graduated.

Even though official government papers said otherwise.

That's government for you, though.

Even Miles was presented a Super-Suit.

Crunch

You should have seen the smile on his face.

Then, (and I think this was just for the sake of a good laugh) they named me team Captain.

Captain Crunch.

They all saluted me and said 'Aye, Aye, Captain Crunch!'.

To top it off Gene had bought numerous kinds of Captain Crunch cereal for us to have for supper.

Really though, everything was going to be a team effort. We loaded up in our big awesome van and set off for the great nothingness that is the UP.

I say 'nothingness' in the best possible way.

There is literally nothing there except a lot of small towns and woods and lakes.

It's a beautiful place, just not much there as far as your normal tourist trap destinations.

Ever been to Niagara falls?

Fantastic place. Way too many people.

So at last we reached the sleepy town of Curtis, Michigan.

It was a funny town, one that still had VCR and video rentals on the side of one building and every store had hand written receipts. The entire town could be driven through in a minute or two, and it only took this long because of the speed limit.

We stopped for supper on the way through at a small pizza joint, which had one guy working in it. I felt a little bad when we ordered 19 pizzas, but we had to eat something.

It was either that or buy 100 packs of hot-dogs.

The good thing was we had 12 people with us this time, so it didn't look *as* strange.

After that we got out of town to Curtis Lake Campground.

Small campground with spots for campers and a number of cabins,

Tyler Svec

all of which were quickly occupied by us.

We looked out on the lake and noted the three islands in the distance, it was difficult to tell which island would have a house on it, but we decided we would scope out the islands the next morning.

We all had a good time and held the annual Amanda and Victoria S'more Eating Contest. Then just for fun I threw Amanda in the lake.

That kind of led into everyone throwing everyone else in the lake. We all ended up soaked.

Except for Mikayla that is.

But her Super-Power is still kind of freaky to me.

The next morning had us splitting into 3 different groups, each heading to a different island to see what was there. I was in the group checking out the middle of the three islands, and it was also the furthest away.

Sure enough, there it was. A small red house sitting in the middle of the small island.

And let me tell you, the Svec's were not kidding about seagull infested.

There had to be 50 million seagulls.

Did you know they nested on the ground?

You could have the easiest Easter Egg hunt on the face of the earth if you went to this island.

They're kind of speckled eggs.

They looked like Mint Chocolate chip ice cream.

Needless to say, if this was in fact the home of Wyatt Dyrt he was probably forced to abandon the place because of all the seagulls.

That night we carefully planned out everything. Due to the fact that we had to take kayaks to get to the cabin in the first place, we were a little limited on what we could take with us. In fact, as far as special weapons (which Bart had in abundance) we could take nothing.

Crunch

Turns out his Super-Power was that he could create new unique weapons that were disguisable.

So even though he was a 'janitor,' he had created some pretty awesome stuff in his day.

We went to sleep, not knowing what tomorrow would bring.

We woke before the crack of dawn, each of us donning our new super-suits and heading out towards the shore where our kayaks were waiting.

You might think we were quite an unusual sight standing on the shore in our Super-Suits.

But the one who looked the weirdest was Gene.

No super-suit for him because he wasn't a Super-Hero.

He looked like James Bond, though.

Freak.

We stepped back and waited as Brent, Victoria, and Amanda stepped up to the shore. Between the heating of the water and cooling of the air they were able to form an unusually thick cloud of fog that covered the lake as far as we could see.

Now we were invisible.

We got into our Kayaks and set off into the water.

Kirra navigated for us as the fog was so thick that we could hardly see the hand in front of our face. We even tied our Kayaks together, so we wouldn't get separated.

Finally we reached the shore of the seagull-infested island.

It was quiet.

Even the seagulls were asleep.

We carefully pulled our boats ashore and made our way through the elaborate maze of seagull eggs till we reached the small cabin.

The door was locked.

Not for long. Ethan punched that door so hard it didn't know what had hit it.

Because it was a door, and they don't know things like that.

We got in and we couldn't see anything. After a moment or two of teasing us mercilessly Gene pulled out a small flashlight to light up the cabin.

Then we found the light-switch, that had been literally right next to the door as we walked in.

Gene teased us some more.

To our surprise though the switch worked and soon the cabin came to life with lights.

Inside it was mostly undisturbed, a paper from fifteen years ago sitting on the table along with a coffee mug that must have been just as old.

For the next twenty minutes we carefully went through all the rooms, looked under every piece of furniture and looked behind anything we could, for a trap door or a clue that would lead us closer to finding the Eraser.

But for the moment we were defeated. We sat down on the old couches and sofas, each lost in our own thoughts until Bart suggested that we search the rest of the small island for anything else that might be able to hold the Eraser. After all it would be a perfectly bad move to put it in a house when that would likely be the first thing that people searched.

We headed back outside and I considered for a moment that the seagulls had intentionally been put on this island just to keep people from going on it.

Five minutes later Bart came running towards us, having found a trapdoor on the forest floor some hundred feet from the back of the house. Soon we all were gathered and sure enough there was a wooden trap door as plain as day.

Crunch

As team 'Captain,' I got the first honor of opening it and leading the way into whatever was waiting for us. I pulled that trap door up, feeling like Indiana Jones on the hunt for some great historical artifacts.

In this case it was the Eraser.

What was revealed when I opened the door was a long shaft that went straight into the ground. A ladder was mounted to the side. Without hesitating I started down the ladder, and soon everyone else had joined me down on the bottom.

We had gone down probably 40 feet and were now were staring at a technological marvel like I've never seen before.

Lasers were everywhere. We could easily pick out heat seeking sensors and other intricate death traps that littered the floor.

But alas, if we could get through everything ahead of us in the center of the room we could have the Mustachio-mobile.

That's right. A car.

An ugly car.

Whoever had designed the bunker must have seen way to many treasure hunting movies. It sat in the middle of the room with a giant spotlight directly overhead, as if it was a shrine to the late great Mustachio . . . who happened to be in the room with us.

Kind of ironic.

Naturally of course all the boys thought it was amazing that there was a car in the bunker. The girls were like, *'We came all this way for a car?'*

I kind of agreed with the girls on that one.

For one thing it was all white, and everyone knows white is a very boring color. Give us some red! Or better yet orange! Something that pops!

And then of course it was an SUV. It wasn't something cool like a Mustang, a Corvette, or a Lamborghini.

Tyler Svec

Come to think about it, we should have just had Miles turn into something antique. Then I would've gotten excited. Make it a 69 Charger, and then it would be cool.

But Alas, we did not think of this at the time.

We found out later, but there was nothing truly unique about the Mustachio-mobile. Save for the over-sized grill to make it look like it had a mustache.

The boys for the most part didn't care, though they were a little bummed, having seen several movies where all this stuff is in a car. Like James Bond or the Bat-mobile, or something of the sort.

But seriously have you ever logistically thought of building a 'bat-mobile'? There are some things you see in the movies that would be completely unrealistic to think that you would be able to put that into a car.

Just one of the reasons that Bruce Wayne and the whole concept of Batman is lame.

Not that Iron Man is much better.

But at least, to his credit, Tony Stark actually builds his own stuff, where Bruce Wayne just takes everyone else's work and makes it look cool.

But to that point, they are the only two who really have a way to die, where as so many Super-Hero's possess God like powers that leaves them invincible for the most part.

Sorry. rant over.

Okay, I'm not that sorry, because it's true and truth hurts sometimes. It especially hurts if you like Batman.

So yes, Iron Man > Batman.

But, for the record . . .

Lego Batman > Iron Man & Batman.

Because Lego Batman's awesome . . . because he's 'Batman!' And

Crunch

it's Lego's. Who doesn't love Legos?

Seriously, one of the best things about being a father is being able to buy Lego's and no one bats an eye at you.

On another note why isn't there a Lego Iron Man? In short, it's because 'Batman' as a concept is so boring, he needs Lego to make him marketable.

Because obviously Lego Iron Man would blow everything right out of the water.

RIP Batman.

Maybe in the future they'll make a Lego "Crunch." That would be cool.

Anyway, now we found this car, and we concluded that there must be something unique about it. The only question now was how to get it out of here and take it home with us.

That was a bit tricky.

As far as the defenses around the car is concerned, that was like a walk in a park.

Que an overly excited Bailey. She's smiling like a school girl who has learned the world's greatest secret. She happily skipped to the far side of the room to an electrical box. She didn't have to cross any of the defense mechanisms along the way.

'Hello, Electrical Box! How'd you like to meet your new worst enemy...me!' Bailey said with a sadistic laugh. Bart also rushed out with one of his weapons. She pulled open the cover and stepped back. She held her hand out and Bart extended his weapon. In unison they both unleashed untold amounts of electricity in the box, frying everything to a crisp. The laser system went off and everything when black, except the single spotlight over the Mustachio-mobile.

Which was now unprotected.

There were a few things we didn't see coming when finally we

Tyler Svec

could get to the Mustachio-mobile. The first was that there seemed to be some very specialized security features on the vehicle that would prevent us from starting it and driving it away . . . which led us to the second problem. How do we get the car out of the bunker when there's no way to drive it out?

Finally after much talk and debate, we figured out a good way to do it. First things first, we went back to shore and we rented a trailer. Then I took Amanda and Victoria to a hotel an hour and a half away. With them out of the picture we prepared to return to the island, under the cover of darkness.

So night came and we rowed out to the island once again. Brent froze the lake so hard it started snowing. Dumped about five inches on it. We all worked together to remove the dirt on top of the bunker and then we let Ethan and Nathan at it. Ethan easily punched his way through the bunker and then as though it was nothing more than a pebble, Nathan picked up the Mustachio-mobile and walked it across the frozen lake, put it on our trailer, and took it home with us.

That's when we got another big surprise.

# Chapter 11

It took us nearly three weeks to get into the Mustachio-mobile and it didn't happen at all how we would have expected. We did all consider using our Super-Powers to get the car open, but with no one to undo what we were doing that could very well destroy the ugly vehicle and make it impossible to learn the secret that had to be inside.

I sometimes have a hard time with vehicles. When I had just learned to drive I had gotten upset about something. I slammed the hood shut with such force that the hood crunched down to a pebble size, all the while proceeding to go through the engine block.

Thus destroying the engine.

Don't even ask me to change the light bulbs in cars. That's just a bad idea.

After much analysis we realized that the car had a 'normal' security system that worked on facial identification, and thanks to Keirra we were able to confirm that the ignition system was hooked up to a similar feature.

Amanda and I knew instantly what needed to be done.

And it wasn't going to be pretty . . .

Tyler Svec

To be fair, there was nothing wrong with our plan except that it would bring back some serious PTSD.

The first clue that this plan would be needed was that the lock for the Mustachio-mobile, was first and foremost a fingerprint reader. So therefore, unless you were in the 'system' you would not be able to get inside.

Unless you were Mustashio, himself. AKA Miles Winkle.

Now this posed a few problems for us from an...ethical standpoint.

How much do we tell him?

Would he freak out if he knew?

The answer to all of those questions was that most likely it would scar him for life if he knew. So we didn't tell him.

We just told him the legends and stories of the great Mustachio.

After we told him a few of the tales that we remembered, Miles screwed his face up and said, *'Man that guy has some serious issues.'*

Right on, brother! Right on!

To put this whole theory to the test we had all the kids (just to be fair) try the fingerprint reader.

It was like a carnival ride. I've never seen them get in line so fast.

The only other time they had moved with such speed was when I announced I was going to Sam's Club for the sole purpose of buying cereal.

I know it sounds ridiculous, but I wanted Captain Crunch.

I love the Captain Crunch with the little berries in it.

Now, they even have it with little marshmallows in it!

They are amazing, but at the same time a major disappointment. It used to be a unique thing to Lucky Charms. now ever single cereal is either "Coco" or has marshmallows.

Someone is lacking in the creative marketing department.

But who cares? It is delicious!

Crunch

And of course I let all the kids pick out a box, and coming from Sam's Club, they weren't small boxes, they were flippin' huge boxes.

Did I mention this was a year ago?

Because it was.

Anyway . . . I digest.

Dirgress, sorry.

Darn spell check . . . digress.

I digress . . . moving on!

So the kids were trying their fingerprints out and just for show Amanda, Gene, Bart and I gave it a go as well. Then finally Miles reached the front and put his thumb on the reader.

We held our breath and then, a light flashed, a buzzer buzzed the lock popped open.

Cheering all around.

He opened up the door and a very fake automated voice says *'Welcome, Mustachio!'* .

Then, from behind all of us, the cat Mustachio running faster than I've ever seen him jumps into the front seat of the car.

I don't recall ever having seen that cat run at all.

It was a historic moment.

I desperately wanted to slam the door shut and break the thumb reader.

Relax! I wouldn't do that.

Miles jumps in the car, which amazingly has the keys inside it. He tries to start it but nothing happens.

It was very anticlimactic.

But as I already told you there was nothing unique about the inside of the car. Except for two things. The seat and steering wheels had very specific sensors which proved to be exactly what we had predicted. Much to our horror.

But I'll get to that in a second.

The kids thought the car was the greatest thing to ever be built because it was a stick-shift, and it had a tape player. Although they had no idea what a tape was.

But to make a long story short, the sensors on the seat and steering wheel were also linked to Mustachio as we had known him. There seemed to even be some kind of facial recognition feature to it.

Basically we had to teach Miles Winkle, how to be Mustachio. We had to tell him how to walk, how to hold himself, and even we had to make a ridiculously big mustache to put on his top lip.

We even went as far as giving him the white suit and hat, which wasn't too much of a hard sell seeing he still had an affinity for white.

Though he hated the large mustache.

All in all, Miles had about three weeks of Mustachio training before we thought he was ready.

So once again we were graced by the presence of a skinny Boss Hog, who would hopefully fool all the sensors and maybe, just maybe we'd be able to find the Eraser and destroy it before memories returned, if they were going to return at all.

This time, he sat down in the seat, turned the key and instantly the Mustachio-mobile started.

Cheering again.

Then Mustachio the cat jumped in, stepped on a button on the middle console (that we hadn't seen up to that point) and the automated voice announced . . .

'Welcome Mr. Stash . . .executing Dash to the Stash sequence in three, two, one!"

Now we probably should've yanked Miles out of the Mustashio-mobile before it got to one, but we wanted to see what happened.

To our wonder and surprise, the door shut and locked itself,

Crunch

rockets came out from the side of the Mustachio-mobile, lifted it fifty feet off the ground, and then in the blink of an eye was gone with a brilliant flash of light.

Gene looks at us and said exactly what all of us were thinking . . . "Oops."

Chapter 12

We stood there looking up at the sky for a good thirty seconds, wondering if what we had seen had actually happened. We kept waiting, and waiting for him to reappear like Marty Mcfly in the Delorean.

But it didn't happen, and a week later we were no closer to figuring out where he had gone.

Mikayla was of course devastated by the love of her life being launched into space.

Not that he was actually in space, but you know what I'm talking about.

All of us spent countless nights staying up late, reading through old files and calling old contacts to get or find any information about where the great Mustachio had lived back then.

Finally we found something. It was a lead, not much of a lead but it was the best we had.

We managed to find a cousin of Mustachio's great uncle two times removed on his mother's side. She said a relative had mentioned once coming to an abandoned mansion in the middle of nowhere.

Crunch

And that nowhere was in Cooladdi, Australia.

Super small town, almost nonexistent.

To Mustachio's credit, it was a pretty smart place to put his lair, if it was there.

The next day we had packed our things and were off to Australia on the cheapest coach air package you could buy. We had ten layovers and took three days to get there.

But, hey, we did it on budget!

Between Mikayla and Amanda it was clear this was going to be a very good trip. It was actually the first time we had been back to Australia since our honeymoon and Amanda was itching to take us all over and show us the sights.

We told her we would, after we found Miles.

It had briefly crossed my mind that perhaps Miles Winkle had played us and he had jetted himself off to his secret lab to once again wreck havoc on the world.

But I hoped that wasn't the case.

We made it to the town and then walked to the other side of the town in thirty seconds.

We asked around, which didn't take long, because there weren't many people.

Finally one of the people said, they knew of an old abandoned mansion that was just twenty miles east to the town. We thanked the man and Gene left him a generous tip.

We headed out of town and with relative ease found the place we were looking for. It was obvious and impossible to miss. First we came to a large gate and over the gate was a cast iron handlebar mustache.

That was all we needed to see.

We pulled out our super suits and as quickly as we could, when you only have cars to get changed in, got into our Super Suits.

Tyler Svec

Now we were ready to save the day.

We no more than got one foot inside the rusty Mustashio gate when hundreds, if not thousands, of small little gun turrets revealed themselves out of the ground.

We were covered in thousands of red little dots and an automated voice that said, *'You move! You die!'*

I laughed and held my hand out in front of me (trying to look cool). A moment later they had been crunched to the size of a mouse. The bullets were even smaller and bounced off us as though they were little pebbles.

Just for fun Bailey EMP'd all of them and then we all had our fun torturing the defenseless gun turrets with our various Super-Powers. Once we got bored from doing that, we continued down the driveway until we reached at last the great mansion of Mustachio!

The mansion was of course white and we weren't at all surprised when Brent mentioned that from the air it probably looked like a big mustache.

There in the front yard was a crashed and mangled Mustachio-mobile, which did little to ease the emotions of a heart broken Mikayla.

I, on the other hand, was thinking about Back to the Future.

Because this totally fit. He takes the car, the car gets broken, he runs into himself and has to convince himself to fix the car, but can't which is why he's been missing so long...

Sorry, but Great Scott! This is Heavy!

I always wonder what was heavy?

In this case the Mustachio-Mobile would've been heavy.

Anyhow . . . after quickly surveying both the Mustashio-Mobile and the surrounding grounds, Kierra was able to confirm that he and the cat had made it out of the car just fine. In fact the tracks said they had gone into the house.

Crunch

I'm not quite sure how she could see it, but I suppose the x-ray powers probably helped some.

Mikayla ran up to the front door and began to knock.

To everyone's relief the door was opened by none other than Miles Winkle!

Mikayla, of course, threw herself into his arms, not giving him a moment to speak, which as a dad was a little weird, but at this point she had thought he was dead for the past month. So I didn't really care too much.

Finally Miles gets us all inside and explained that the car had not landed right and therefore it was broken and he couldn't get back.

Now, you could definitely tell that he was a rookie at this sort of thing, because with his superpower, he totally could've turned something into something old and valuable to raise the money to get home.

But it was his first time, so we didn't give him to much grief.

Inside the house was spotless and conveniently well stocked, and Miles explained that it seemed to restock itself, which was rather handy.

When we asked what he had been up to the past month he led us to an underground level of the mansion. There in the middle of a great lab was a table with hundreds, if not thousands, of small pieces sitting on top of it.

And also Mustachio the cat.

To the side of the table was a large book and then it became painstakingly clear to us.

These were the instructions that came with the Eraser, and Miles Winkle in his not remembering state was trying to put it together. So we sat down and built it together, although Amanda and I did conveniently crunch and melt several key parts that would prevent the

Tyler Svec

Eraser from ever being used again.

When finally we were done we had a mostly complete Eraser that would never work again. There was great speculation and conversations about what it would do.

We just said we weren't going to find out.

So after that was all done, we decided it was time to head home. We had already contacted Miles's parents.

Who I forgot to mention until now. They had been thoroughly briefed and told the true story after we told them that their son had vanished in a fashion like he had.

It was when we got back to the small little town that we were met by a man in a dark suit. The rest of us kind of freaked out a little but it became clear that it was somehow a friend of Gene's.

But he had the dark sunglasses and the black SUV with three other people standing behind him. I did have to laugh a little, if they were here to arrest us, we would totally whoop their butts.

Gene embraced the guy and they started laughing and talking as though they were old friends. The man was introduced as Roger and turned out to be a cousin of Gene's.

We all returned to the Mustachio-mansion so we could talk privately for a while. It turns out that Roger wanted to hire all of us for a job.

He didn't tell us specifically but he took all of us on a trip to an undisclosed location, a small village of about twenty people. In the middle was one of the most awesome sights I've ever seen.

In the middle of the village square entertaining the crowd was as a tall kid, plenty scary to look at. He had tattoos up and down his arms, muscles coming out of everywhere! Freaky-looking hair, and he wore a tank-top and bandanna.

He was introduced as Nick Selma, but we all knew that it was none

Crunch

other than the Snake King! He even had the eye patch!

He was apparently a street performer in the Australian Outback. Dazzling people with his tricks, which based on the few conversations I heard, made most people think he was possessed by something.

I was just glad to see the Snake King again. He was still soft spoken, but he could still turn himself into a fire shooting, mind piercing, acid trailing snake that will strike terror into anyone.

As it turns out, the governments of the world were starting to have a bit of a problem as there was an increasing number of Super-Heroes who were starting to show up, but had no idea of how to actually be a Super-Hero.

In short we were offered a job, to teach these kids, while having all expenses paid for by the government. We talked about it later that night and then shook hands on it the next day.

So then we had a tour of Australia, led by my awesome wife, Amanda. She even went as far as showing us the house where she had grown up.

I watched her parents carefully but still, none of them seemed to remember anything. Visiting there did have a few questions pop up that we had never thought to prepare an answer for such as...

'So, what happened to your parents?'

'Did they die?'

'It's really too bad we've grown up without grandparents. You know grandparents supposedly give good gifts.'

It was kind of an awkward situation and we answered as truthfully as we could. We told them that we hoped we could see them again some day.

Then when it was finally time to leave, Roger arranged a first class private jet to get us home, and it must have been a super jet, because it took only three hours to get there.

Tyler Svec

Finally we all touched down in Traverse City, Michigan, and went back to our house in Interlochen.

Chapter 13

It was almost a year until we noticed the first hints of the Eraser effects wearing off.

It seems my dad was having memories of the first time he had met my mom, Bailey, and couldn't quite make sense of it all.

So, knowing it was time, Amanda and I sat everyone down and told them the truth of what had happened so many years ago, and the implications of what had taken place on Curtis Lake and at the Mustachio-mansion.

However, that being said, Mr. Winkle seemed still totally oblivious to any memories, so we didn't tell him anything regarding him.

Him being Mustachio.

Which one could argue that he wasn't Mustachio.

Not now, anyway.

He no longer wore a mustache as Mikayla had voiced a distaste for it, and as she said *'I prefer not to kiss a big fuzzy caterpillar.'*

Hence the mustache had vanished.

It took everyone a bit of adjusting and even if you ask me I will tell you that not everything turned out quite the way I thought it would.

Tyler Svec

It was strange in some ways to see what memories came back and which memories didn't. Because although all of our parents seemed to have some inclination that they were married at one point in time, all the memories didn't come rushing back.

Instead it was probably another two years before all the memories that had been once shared between all of them were fully back. They didn't physically catch up to where their memories were, so they still looked like our kids, even though . . .

They kind of were.

And still as time went on, Mustachio remembered nothing. In fact, our parents had no recollection of anyone ever named Mustachio.

They certainly never had any connection in their memories that placed the infamous name with the person who was now Miles Winkle.

This was for the best no doubt, and between Amanda, Bart, Gene and all his super secret government friends we made sure that nothing linking the two of them would ever be found again.

So eventually the day came when weddings were in order, but to our surprise Mikayla and Miles were the first to tie the knot.

It was a big occasion to say the least.

Even saw Mustachio the cat as the ring bearer.

He was on a leash.

Led by Mr. Gents himself.

It was kind of pathetic.

We gave them the cat as a wedding gift.

He's still alive if you can believe that. Still stupid, but alive . . . and kind of likable.

But I never said that publicly, mind you!

After the wedding they moved not too far away.

Like literally across the street.

It was another year after that till our parents came forward and

Crunch

wanted to get married to each other as they had been.

This was a slight problem for us, politically speaking.

Obviously, it was totally fine. They were once married, they are technically our parents. So what's the problem?

The biggest problem was of course that only the Svec's knew about the situation. Therefore to anyone else it would look like we were letting our kids partake in rather scandalous relationships.

To solve the problem, we gave them all permission to marry, but they would have to have very small ceremonies and then move elsewhere for a couple of years.

Hopefully when they returned everyone would've forgotten.

So that's what happened. We all met down by the courthouse and both sets of parents were remarried and moved to different parts of the country for a year or two.

But then we all ended up back together in good old Interlochen.

Thankfully, for the sake of our own sanity, our parents never had any more children . . . but they very easily fell into the role of grandparents/aunts and uncles who looked like they had found the fountain of youth, when Mikayla and Miles had their first child.

But out of all the memories I can recall, there's one that is in some ways more meaningful to me than many others I've shared with you.

I was sitting on our back porch and it was just me and Nathan (my dad). Somewhere in the course of our conversation he looks at me and says . . .

'Son. I'm proud of you.' I smiled, knowing that I could say the same thing back to him.

And I did.

But those words have power, and in that moment I knew that although God had called Amanda and I to an unusual life, it was the right thing to do.

Tyler Svec

I've always found that looking at things in retrospect always allows you to see things more clearly. You can see God's hand moving and guiding you through everything.

How he puts people in your life like Gene, or Bart and each other.

If you trust in God . . . I can't say your life will be easy or perfect.

But it will be fulfilling.

Now I'm sure you're probably wondering about what life looked like after the great Mustachio trip right? Well, here are some highlights.

Starting with my parents Bailey and Nathan, they both use their powers in interesting ways. Bailey is a cop and has gotten a reputation for miraculously catching the bad guys when they're in a high speed chase.

She just gives their car a nice EMP blast.

Nathan works for a construction company and can lift anything you want.

Once when they were on an assignment together in a super secret place, an entire building had to be evacuated and all the doors were locking themselves. In rushes my dad to use his Super-Strength to keep the door open, allowing everyone to get out free and clear.

Kierra works in the medical profession and to anyone who doesn't know she's a Super-Hero she does the regular x-rays, though she turns the machine on only so she doesn't get any questions.

Ethan has become the unofficial body guard of first time recruits. He goes with them on their first mission and provides backup as he wields his mighty 'Fist of silence.'

At least that's what he calls it.

As far as our actual biological kids are concerned, Brent (the Iceman) continues to put a new meaning to the whole phrase 'when Hell freezes over' because for him, it basically does.

Crunch

One bad guy we were chasing went right into the heart of a volcano, where his secret lab was. That would've stopped most people in their tracks, but not Brent.

In a matter of seconds the volcano looked like a snow cone.

Needless to say the bad guy was caught.

Mikayla has struggled a bit to keep from laughing when the bad guys get duct tape to restrain her. Then she proceeds to mock them as they grow increasingly frustrated with the 'tape' that isn't sticking to her.

Miles always goes with her on assignment and the two of them never take any pay, not matter how small. But usually to pay for their own way, Mustachio or (Miles) effortlessly turns a pointless object into something worth a lot of money.

And last but not least you have Victoria who got locked in a restaurant's walk in freezer and then left for three days.

When she was found, the entire freezer was broken down and instead the place had turned into a sauna.

And she had her choice of any of the foods, which had come unfrozen so she was totally fine.

Bart ended up taking a job at the new bad guy jail. He was the toughest, but still kindest corrections officer you'd ever meet, using all of his various tools that were in his mop bucket.

Gene kept the government people happy and was always finding new people for us to train.

Amanda and I stay busy traveling and training all the new Super-Heroes who arise on the world. It's been fun and rewarding for us to be in an advisory role and be able to guide the new Super-Heroes in a way that might eventually lead them to God.

For years it had kind of annoyed me that Super-Heroes rarely thought about God.

Tyler Svec

They thought about themselves and how awesome they were.

It can hardly be blamed on them, because that is what society taught them.

But a few asked the question of where did my Super-Powers come from?

God gives us all Super-Powers. They may not be 'crunching' or anything like that, but you do have some ability that God has given you and will use for his glory, if you so choose to *let* him.

Life has been great, and I can't wait to see what God has in store for us next.

That's our story.
I'm Walter Braymend ('Crunch')
And that is the life of a Super-Hero!

The Real "Mustachio" the cat...